The Adventures of Brer Rabbit

The Adventures of Brer Rabbit

BY JOEL CHANDLER HARRIS

illustrated by Frank Baber

RAND McNALLY & COMPANY
Chicago · New York · San Francisco

Contents

The stories in this book were selected and adapted by Ruth Spriggs, with the help of Stephen Bates and Sarah White.

SBN 528-82300-0

Printed in the United States of America by Rand McNally and Company

Library of Congress Catalog Card Number: 80-52016

Introduction

The Brer Rabbit stories are folktales that were handed down from generation to generation by black slaves on the plantations of the South. Before television or radio were invented, storytelling was an important art and although the adventures of Brer Rabbit were not written down they were widely known.

Towards the end of the last century, Joel Chandler Harris, an Atlanta newspaperman, traveled around the South, listening to the storytellers and writing down what he heard. He used the stories in articles and later published several books. In the most famous of these, *Uncle Remus* and *Nights with Uncle Remus*, the stories are told to a little boy by a former slave, Uncle Remus. Every night the little boy makes his way to the old man's cabin, fascinated by the character of Brer Rabbit and always begging for a new adventure.

Where did the richly humorous tales of Brer Rabbit come from? Joel Chandler Harris was convinced---as are many present-day scholars---that they were originally African, brought to America long ago by the slaves. Whatever their origin, the crafty, idle, mischief-making rabbit and his wily old acquaintances Brer Fox and Brer Wolf are characters people all over the world will recognize---among their human friends and neighbors.

The stories in Mr. Harris's books were written in heavy dialect and are full of words and spellings that are difficult for today's readers to understand. In this edition they have been retold in modern English. Every effort has been made to retain the spirit and humor of the original versions and we hope that in this way they will be read and appreciated by more and more children. We are sure that parents will enjoy reading them, too.

Brer Rabbit goes out to dinner

Brer Rabbit and Brer Fox were old enemies.
They were always trying to trick each other
and always getting into all kinds of trouble.
One day after an especially bad week when
Brer Fox had been doing all he could to
catch Brer Rabbit and Brer Rabbit had
been doing everything he could to avoid
being caught, Brer Fox made a new plan.

He had only just finished working out the details when Brer Rabbit came loping up the road looking as plump and as pleased with himself as a horse in a field of oats.

"Hold on there, Brer Rabbit," said Brer Fox.

"No time now, Brer Fox," said Brer Rabbit, quickening his pace a little.

"I've something to discuss with you, Brer Rabbit," said Brer Fox.

"All right but you'd better just shout out from where you're standing now. I seem to have caught a whole fur full of fleas from somewhere. I'd keep a safe distance if I were you."

"Well," said Brer Fox, beginning to feel a bit itchy in spite of the distance between them, "I saw Brer Bear yesterday and he was complaining that you and I just can't seem to live like friends and neighbors. I told him I'd have a serious word with you. Perhaps it really is time we worked something out."

Brer Rabbit sat down on the road and scratched his ear with his back foot. Then he said rather dubiously: "We might just do that, Brer Fox. Suppose you drop around tomorrow and take dinner with me. We're nothing special at our house you know but I expect Mrs. Rabbit and the kids can scramble round and fix up something to fill your stomach."

"That's mighty civil of you, Brer Rabbit," said Brer Fox.

"Then I'll depend on you," said Brer Rabbit.

Next day Brer Rabbit and his wife crept out before it was light and raided a nearby garden for cabbages, fat ears of sweet corn and tender asparagus shoots. They set to work to fix a really good dinner.

Just about dinner time one of the little rabbits who was playing in the backyard came running and tumbling in through the door.

"Mom, oh Mom, it's Mr. Fox. I saw Mr. Fox coming down the path."

Then Brer Rabbit took all the little rabbits by the ears and sat them down sternly

in the corner. He and Mrs. Rabbit stood by the table—all laid for dinner—and waited for a knock on the door. They waited and they waited but there was no knock on the door and no sound on the path outside.

After a little while Brer Rabbit tiptoed over to the door and peeped out. There, sticking out from the corner of the wall was the very tip of a bushy tail. As Brer Rabbit stood looking, the tip twitched and flicked out of sight. Brer Rabbit shut the door very quickly and sat thinking for a moment.

"Brer Fox, my old pal," he said, "there's more to this than meets the eye. But come to the table, children. Mr. Fox or no Mr. Fox, we'll have the best dinner we've eaten for a long time."

Next day Brer Fox sent a message explaining that he had been too sick to call on Brer Rabbit the day before. Instead, he invited Brer Rabbit to come to have dinner at his house.

"Suits me," said Brer Rabbit. So just at the middle of the day Brer Rabbit brushed his fur, smoothed his whiskers, straightened his ears and sauntered down to Brer Fox's house. As he came up to the door he could hear someone groaning inside. Looking in through the half open door he saw Brer Fox sitting in a rocking chair wrapped in a blanket. He was rocking backwards and forwards, moaning and looking very weak and sorry for himself.

Brer Rabbit stood cautiously in the doorway and looked around. There was no sign of any food. The roasting dish lay on the table with, close by, a sharp carving knife.

"Hmm," thought Brer Rabbit. "I smell a trick in this." Aloud he said, "Looks as if you're going to have chicken for dinner, Brer Fox."

"Chickens are nice and fresh and tender," said Brer Fox faintly.

"All cooked and ready then, is it?" asked Brer Rabbit.

"Ready when you are, Brer Rabbit," said Brer Fox, licking his lips and quite forgetting to look sick.

Brer Rabbit still stood in the doorway and pulled his whiskers in a thoughtful kind of a way.

"You haven't any onions, have you, Brer Fox?" he asked. "My stomach's so sensitive these days that I just can't digest chicken unless it's seasoned up with onions. I'll just go and pick you some."

And with that Brer Rabbit leaped out of the door and dodged among the bushes. He waited there to see what Brer Fox would do next. He did not have long to wait. As soon as Brer Fox realized that Brer Rabbit suspected a trick he flung off the blanket and crept out of the house, stalking through the long grass.

"Are you there, Brer Rabbit? Have you found the onion patch? It's over here."

Brer Rabbit was over the fence in a couple of bounds.

"I'm not that stupid," he said to himself. "You'll not catch me that way." Aloud he called: "I'll just leave the onions on this post here. Better come and get them while they're fresh. And hurry back to the chicken—you don't want it to get cold now do you?"

Brer Rabbit and the tar baby

One day soon after Brer Rabbit had tricked Brer Fox out of his dinner, Brer Fox had an idea. He hid himself away in the old shed at the end of the yard and made a large doll out of an old suit stuffed with straw and dry leaves. He made a head out of a pumpkin, painted on eyes and teeth and stuck a carrot on the front for a nose. Lastly, he mixed a bucket full of tar and turpentine and dipped the whole doll into it so that it was thickly coated with black, sticky liquid.

"That's just about the prettiest tar baby I ever saw," he said in a satisfied voice.

Carrying it carefully away from his fur, he crept down to the road and propped the tar baby up among the weeds by the bank. Then he slunk away into the bushes, flattened his body close against the ground and lay low, waiting, with only his eyes moving as he looked eagerly up and down the road.

Brer Fox did not have long to wait. Very soon Brer Rabbit came trotting down the road—*lippity-clippity, clippity-lippity*—as cheerful as could be.

Brer Fox lay low in the bushes.

When Brer Rabbit caught sight of the tar baby he reared up on his back legs in surprise, then stood still and stared at the tar baby. The tar baby stood still and stared back at him. Brer Fox lay low in the bushes.

"Morning, Mister," said Brer Rabbit in a friendly way. "Nice weather we're having this morning, isn't it?"

The tar baby said nothing.

"And how are you today?" went on Brer Rabbit, still nice and friendly.

The tar baby said nothing. Brer Fox lay low in the bushes but he winked one of his crafty eyes very slowly.

"Well how are you then?" said Brer Rabbit, rather crossly. "Are you deaf or something? Because if that's your problem I can shout more loudly."

The tar baby said nothing.

"You're stuck up, that's what it is," shouted Brer Rabbit. "And I'm just the one to cure you of that."

Brer Fox gave a sort of low, rumbling chuckle in his stomach. Still the tar baby said nothing.

"I'll teach you how to speak to respectable people if it's the last thing I do," said Brer Rabbit. "If you don't say 'How are you' like a gentleman, I'll just have to do it for you."

The tar baby stood still and silent. Brer Fox lay low in the bushes. Brer Rabbit took a step nearer the tar baby and asked again in a menacing voice: "How are you, Mister?"

The tar baby said nothing.

Quick as a flash, Brer Rabbit drew back his fist and—*blip*—he landed a punch on the side of the tar baby's head. And that was Brer Rabbit's first mistake! His fist hit the tar baby right on the side of the head and there it stayed, stuck fast in the thick tar. The tar baby went on standing there—and Brer Fox lay low in the bushes.

"Just you let go of me. If you don't let go this minute I'll hit you again," shouted Brer Rabbit and—*blip*—he hit the tar baby with his other fist. The tar baby shook a little as the blow landed and Brer Rabbit started to laugh triumphantly. Next minute he realized his left hand was stuck firmly to the other side of the tar baby's head.

"Let me go before I kick you inside out," shrieked Brer Rabbit and, as the tar baby remained quite still, he lashed out at it with first his right foot, then his left. And first his right foot, then his left stuck fast to the tar baby's sticky covering.

At this point Brer Rabbit really lost his temper. He pulled and struggled and pushed and shook the tar baby but nothing he did could free his hands and feet. Finally, in a rage, he butted the tar baby as hard as he could with the side of his head—and stuck fast with his nose twitching half an inch from the tarry coat. Just at that moment Brer Fox sauntered out of his hiding place, looking as innocent as could be.

"Howdy, Brer Rabbit," said Brer Fox casually. "You look sort of stuck up this

morning." Then he gave a great snort of laughter and rolled on the ground and laughed and laughed until he could not laugh any more.

"I expect you'll take dinner with me this evening," he gasped between snorts. "I've laid in a special supply of onions—ha ha ha—and I won't hear any—oh, dear me—excuses. I really can't take no for an answer this time."

After a while, Brer Fox really could not laugh any longer and, gasping for breath he said: "I've really got you now, Brer Rabbit, and about time too. You've been running around getting your own way for too long but it's the end of the track for you now my fine fellow. There you are and there you'll stay while I just get a great big bonfire together. For I'm going to have barbecued rabbit today if it's the last thing I do."

Brer Rabbit's mouth was only a few inches from the tar baby. His head, hands and feet were all stuck fast to the tar. When he spoke he did not sound like the old, cheeky Brer Rabbit at all.

"I don't care what you do to me, Brer Fox," he said very humbly, "as long as you don't throw me into the briar patch over there. Roast me if you like but don't throw me into the briar patch."

"It's so much trouble to get a fire going

out here," said Brer Fox, "that I'll probably have to hang you."

"Hang me as high as you like, Brer Fox," whined Brer Rabbit, "but for heaven's sake don't throw me into the briar patch."

"Fortunately for you I don't have any rope," said Brer Fox. "I suppose I could always drown you."

"Drown me as deep as you like, Brer Fox," said Brer Rabbit, "just as long as you don't throw me into the briar patch."

"Problem is I can't see any water round here deep enough," grumbled Brer Fox. "I guess I'll just have to skin you alive."

"You can skin me, Brer Fox, you can cut me into little pieces and make gloves out of me but please, Brer Fox, I beg you, if you have any pity for a fellow creature—*don't throw me into the briar patch*."

Brer Fox stood in the lane for a minute or two considering what to do. Then his crafty eyes narrowed to fine yellow slits and he crouched low to the ground. Suddenly he leaped at Brer Rabbit, snatched him by the back legs, pulled him off the tar baby and flung him straight over the bank, right into the middle of the briar patch.

There was a great smashing, struggling, splintering noise as Brer Rabbit struck the brambles and Brer Fox, panting from his efforts, trotted up to look what was happening. Everything seemed quiet and still. Brer Fox peered this way and that. Nothing. He sniffed the air. Nothing. He cocked his head on one side to listen. Nothing. Then:

"Hi there, Brer Fox," came a voice from the distance. Brer Fox whirled around. Halfway up the hill, there was Brer Rabbit, sitting cross-legged on a fallen log, combing the tar out of his fur with a twig. Brer Fox knew he had been tricked again. As he slunk away home, Brer Rabbit's mocking voice followed after him down the road.

"I was bred and born in a briar patch, Brer Fox. Bred and born in a briar patch."

As for Brer Rabbit, when he had cleaned the tar off every tangled hair, he skipped off without a care in the world.

Brer Rabbit's race

One day when Brer Rabbit was trotting lippity clippity down the road he saw Brer Terrapin sitting under a tree.

"Are you at home, Brer Terrapin?" asked Brer Rabbit politely, knocking on the top of the terrapin's shell. He knew that sometimes when Brer Terrapin was in a bad mood he might pretend not to be in. But today he poked his head out and they started to have a friendly conversation. After a while they began to talk about how fast the various animals could run.

"I can outrun Brer Fox and Brer Wolf any day," boasted Brer Rabbit. "And of course Brer Bear would not stand a chance against me."

"What about Mrs. Cow?" asked Brer Terrapin.

Brer Rabbit laughed. "Come on, now, be serious, Brer Terrapin. She's hardly any faster than you are yourself. And you must admit you're not exactly the fastest thing on four legs."

Brer Terrapin looked rather cross about this.

"I don't know about that, Brer Rabbit," he said. "I reckon I can give you a good race any day. In fact I'm reasonably sure that I can win."

"What?" Brer Rabbit shrieked with laughter. "You, Brer Terrapin? You give me a good race? If I sowed barley seeds as I went along the whole row would be ripe enough to cut by the time you reached the finishing post."

Brer Terrapin did not even smile. "Brer Rabbit," he said, "you talk too much. I'll not argue with you here but if you arrange a route and a fair judge I'll show you who's right and who's wrong about speed." Muttering "I'll show him the fastest thing on four legs," he drew his head back inside his shell and refused to say another word.

Chuckling at the idea of an easy victory, Brer Rabbit bounded off to ask Brer Buzzard to be judge and to chose a suitable course for the race.

Before long all the arrangements had been made. The race was to be run over five miles and the route was carefully measured off with a post stuck up at every mile along the way. Brer Rabbit chose to run along the road but Brer Terrapin preferred to gallop through the woods along the side. Everyone told him he would get along much faster on the road but old Brer Terrapin knew what he was doing all right.

Then Brer Rabbit went into training, skipping over the ground as gaily as a cricket in June. Old Brer Terrapin stayed quietly in the swamp with his wife and four children. Now Mrs. Terrapin and all the children were just the spitting image of old Brer Terrapin. You would need a magnifying glass to tell one from the other— and even then you might make a mistake.

On the day of the race, Brer Terrapin, his wife and his four children were up before sunrise, making their way to the racecourse. Mrs. Terrapin took her place at the starting post. The youngest child plodded off and hid in the woods beside the first mile post, the second child hid beside the second mile post, the third child beside the third mile post, and the fourth and oldest beside the fourth mile post. Brer Terrapin himself settled down in the woods in sight of the winning post.

As soon as the sun was well up, a crowd of animals began to collect at the start of the race. Judge Buzzard perched on the starting post and there was an excited hum of conversation. At last Brer Rabbit came dancing along. He looked an amazing sight, with ribbons tied around his neck and more ribbons streaming from his ears. He strutted about among the animals, flexing his muscles, running on the spot and generally showing off to anyone who would pay him attention.

Judge Buzzard decided it was time to start and without waiting for the final signal, all the animals rushed away to the finishing post to make sure they were in the best position to cheer the winner home.

"Are you ready, gentlemen?" asked Brer Buzzard.

"Ready," said Mrs. Terrapin in a deep voice.

"Go," cried Brer Buzzard.

Brer Rabbit set off as fast as he could run. Old Mrs. Terrapin crawled steadily towards her home in the swamp. Brer Buzzard rose into the air and skimmed overhead to see that the race was run fairly—but of course even his piercing eyes could not penetrate the woodland undergrowth where, everyone thought, Brer Terrapin was making steady progress.

Just as Brer Rabbit reached the first mile post the youngest terrapin crawled out of the woods and made for the check point. Brer Rabbit came leaping along, still fresh and confident.

"Where are you, Brer Terrapin?" he called out over his shoulder.

"Here I come steaming along," said the youngest terrapin in a deep voice.

Brer Rabbit was glad to find he was ahead but he ran faster than ever—and the youngest terrapin set off for home like his mother.

When he came to the next mile post he saw another terrapin crawling towards it.

"Where are you, Brer Terrapin?" called Brer Rabbit.

"Here I come boiling along," said the second youngest terrapin.

Brer Rabbit ran to the next mile post. A terrapin was just crawling to the post as he panted up. And at the fourth post a terrapin was actually there before him. There was one more mile to go and Brer Rabbit's legs were beginning to feel a little bit tired and his lungs were beginning to hurt. Down at the winning post Brer Terrapin lurked in the shelter of the wood, watching. At last he saw Brer Buzzard sailing along and then he knew that Brer Rabbit was on his way. So he scrambled through the waiting crowd of animals to the winning post and crawled behind it.

Soon enough along came Brer Rabbit. As he came to the post he glanced over his shoulder and, seeing no sign of Brer Terrapin, he shouted: "I've won, I've won! Be my witness, Brer Buzzard, all of you. I've beaten Brer Terrapin. I'm the fastest thing on four legs."

To his surprise the whole crowd burst out laughing and pointing. Brer Terrapin was standing on his short back legs, peering round the winning post.

"If you'll just give me a minute to get my breath back, I'll explain why you're wrong, Brer Rabbit," he said. "But right now I must run off home and eat a bite of breakfast. Winning races gives me quite an appetite."

Brer Rabbit goes riding

Brer Rabbit kept himself to himself for a few days after the tar baby incident to make sure all the tar had rubbed off his hair but before long he was loping around just as if nothing had happened. If there was any difference, he may have looked even more cheeky than before.

One day when his fur was as good as new, Brer Rabbit called on some friends of his, Mr. and Mrs. Possum and their family. Of course everyone had heard the story of the tar baby and the children just could not stop giggling about it. Brer Rabbit sat quiet and dignified while they teased him. Then, leaning back in the chair he crossed his legs comfortably, gave a slow, knowing wink of the eye and said:

"Of course, Brer Fox was my daddy's riding horse for thirty years, maybe even more."

The Possums stopped laughing and began to ask him questions but Brer Rabbit said nothing more.

Next day Brer Fox happened to call on the Possums and when he began to laugh about Brer Rabbit, they told him what Brer Rabbit had said. Brer Fox ground his teeth in rage and looked extremely fierce. Just as he was about to leave he said: "I'm not doubting what you say—but I'll make sure that Brer Rabbit chews up his words and spits them out right here where you can all see it."

Brer Fox made straight for Brer Rabbit's house but when he arrived there Brer Rabbit was expecting him for the door was shut fast. Brer Fox knocked. Nobody answered. So Brer Fox knocked again—*blam blam*. Then Brer Rabbit called out weakly.

"Is that you, Brer Fox? Please run and fetch the doctor for me. That bit of garlic I ate this morning is doing something horrible to my stomach. Please, Brer Fox, run quickly. I'm sure it was poisoned."

"But there's going to be a party up at the Possums'," said Brer Fox, "and I came to fetch you. Everyone is there and I promised I would make you come along. The children say it just won't be a party without Brer Rabbit."

"Oh I'm much too ill," said Brer Rabbit.

"No you're not," said Brer Fox.

"Yes I am, I tell you," said Brer Rabbit.

"And I say you're not," said Brer Fox.

"But I can't walk, Brer Fox. My knees just give way when I stand up."

"Why, then I'll carry you, Brer Rabbit," said Brer Fox, only thinking of how to get Brer Rabbit to the Possums' house.

"How will you carry me?" asked Brer Rabbit.

"In my arms, of course," said Brer Fox.

"Whoever heard of a fox carrying anything in his arms," said Brer Rabbit. "You'll drop me for sure."

"Course I won't," said Brer Fox.

"Course you will," said Brer Rabbit. "I'm only going with you if you carry me on your back."

"If that's the only way you'll come then

that's how I'll carry you," said Brer Fox.

"But I can't ride without a saddle," went on Brer Rabbit.

"I'll get you a saddle."

"And I can't just sit on a saddle and hope for the best. I need a bridle to hold on to."

"No problem, Brer Rabbit. I'll get a bridle right away."

"Better get one with good blinkers or you'll be shying at tree stumps all the way and you'll throw me off."

"Don't worry, Brer Rabbit. That's settled then. I'll give you a ride most of the way and when we get nearby you can get down and walk."

"Done," said Brer Rabbit and Brer Fox ran off to find a saddle and bridle.

Of course Brer Rabbit had guessed the trick Brer Fox was planning to play on him and he was determined to outwit him. By the time he had combed his hair, curled his whiskers and smartened himself up, along came Brer Fox fitted up with a handsome saddle and bridle, looking as pretty as a circus pony. He trotted up to the door and stood there pawing the ground and champing at the bit just like a real horse.

Brer Rabbit mounted and they trotted off.

Brer Fox could not see what was going on behind because of the blinkers but by and by he felt Brer Rabbit raise one of his feet.

"What are you doing back there, Brer Rabbit?" he asked suspiciously.

"Just shortening the left stirrup, Brer Fox," he said.

After a while Brer Rabbit raised his right foot.

"What are you doing now?" asked Brer Fox.

"Just hitching up my pants, Brer Fox."

But all the time Brer Rabbit was putting on a pair of sharp spurs. When they came near to the Possums' house and Brer Fox began to slow down, Brer Rabbit dug the spurs deep into the fox's sides—and how Brer Fox ran!

Mrs. Possum and her children were sitting on the verandah. Instead of stopping at the gate, Brer Rabbit rode Brer Fox right up the garden path. Quick as a flash he dismounted, and tied the reins firmly to the verandah rail and sauntered casually into the house. He shook hands politely, sat down and settled back to smoke a cigar.

"Didn't I tell you Brer Fox was the riding horse in our family?" he said. "Of course he's a bit out of practice at the moment but I'll be able to train him up again all right in a month or so."

Then Brer Rabbit gave a kind of grin and the children began to giggle and Mrs. Possum began to praise the "horse". And poor Brer Fox was hitched fast to the rail and could not do a thing about it at all.

Brer Fox
is tricked again

When the time came for Brer Rabbit to
leave he walked over to Brer Fox, unhitched
the reins, mounted and rode off. Brer Fox
said nothing, just ambled quietly along as if
he did it every day. Brer Rabbit knew
something was going on and was prepared
for just about anything.

As soon as they were out of sight of the
Possums' house, Brer Fox went crazy. He

ripped and roared and he swore and cursed and he snarled and cavorted all over the road. Of course he was trying to fling Brer Rabbit off his back—but he might as well have tried wrestling with his own shadow. Every time he bucked Brer Rabbit stuck the sharp spurs into him. Brer Fox tore up the ground and jumped so high and so quickly that he nearly shook his tail off. Still Brer Rabbit seemed fixed firmly in the saddle. Then Brer Fox lay down on the ground and rolled over and over as fast as he could. At last this unseated Brer Rabbit but by the time Brer Fox was back on his feet Brer Rabbit was tearing through the undergrowth as if he were a racehorse himself!

Brer Fox ran after him, snapping his long sharp teeth at the rabbit's heels. He was just about to close on Brer Rabbit when Brer Rabbit darted inside a hollow forest tree. Brer Fox nearly banged his head on the trunk as he screeched to a stop but Brer Rabbit was safe: the hole was too small for Brer Fox to get into.

Brer Fox lay down on his side to recover his breath and think what to do next. While he was lying there Brer Buzzard came flopping along. When he saw Brer Fox flat out on the ground he hopped nearer.

"Oh dear, Brer Fox is dead. What a pity," he said.

"No I'm not dead," said Brer Fox. "I've got that old rabbit penned up in there and I'm going to get him this time if I have to wait until Christmas."

Brer Buzzard agreed to watch the hole and keep Brer Rabbit inside while Brer Fox went to fetch his axe. Brer Buzzard took up his post to wait. Everything was quiet. After a time Brer Rabbit crept close to the hole and shouted: "Brer Fox, oh Brer Fox."

Brer Fox wasn't there and Brer Buzzard kept quiet. Then Brer Rabbit shouted angrily: "Don't talk if you don't want to then. I know you're there and I don't care. I just want to tell you that I really wish that Brer Buzzard was here."

Brer Buzzard cocked his head to one side and tried to talk like Brer Fox.

"What do you want with Brer Buzzard then?"

"Oh, nothing in particular. It's just that there's the fattest gray squirrel you ever saw in here and if Brer Buzzard was here he'd be glad to get him for his dinner."

"How could Brer Buzzard get him then?" said Brer Buzzard, still trying to sound like Brer Fox.

"Well," said Brer Rabbit, "there's a little hole round the other side of the tree and if Brer Buzzard was here he could stand there and I'd drive the squirrel out to him."

"You drive him out then," said Brer Buzzard. "I'll see that Brer Buzzard gets him."

Then Brer Rabbit began to make a scratching, scrabbling, squealing noise as if he were driving something out. Brer Buzzard rushed round to the other side of the tree to catch the squirrel and Brer Rabbit dashed out of the hole and just flew for home as fast as his four legs would carry him.

Brer Buzzard sat on the other side of the tree waiting for the squirrel to come out. But of course no squirrel came. After a time he began to get rather lonely but he had promised Brer Fox that he would wait and he wanted to see what sort of trick Brer Fox had planned.

Quite soon Brer Fox came galloping back through the woods with his axe.

"How do you think Brer Rabbit is getting on?" asked Brer Fox.

"Oh he's in there," said Brer Buzzard. "He's very quiet though. I expect he's having a nap."

"Then I'm just in time to wake him up," said Brer Fox. And he flung off his coat, spat on his hands and grabbed the axe. He raised it high above his head and brought it down—pow—onto the trunk of the tree. Again and again he swung the axe and each time it hit the trunk, Brer Buzzard stretched his neck, flapped his wings and shouted:

"He's in there, Brer Fox. He's in there." And every time a chip of wood flew off, Brer Buzzard jumped and dodged and put his head on one side shouting: "Yes, there he is,

Brer Fox. I can hear him scratching about in there trying to hide."

Brer Fox chopped away at the tree like a mad fox. When he had chopped most of the way through the trunk he stopped suddenly to get his breath and caught Brer Buzzard laughing at him behind his back. Brer Buzzard stopped as soon as he saw Brer Fox had seen him and began to shout again: "He's in there, Brer Fox, he's in there. I just saw him looking out."

Brer Fox pretended to believe him and ran up to the hole in the tree.

"Come here, Brer Buzzard, quick, come and look. Here's Brer Rabbit's foot hanging down."

Brer Buzzard of course knew very well that Brer Rabbit had escaped and he hopped up to the hole as if he were hopping on hot coals and very cautiously stuck his head inside. No sooner had he done so than Brer

Fox grabbed him. Brer Buzzard flapped his wings and scrambled round as quickly as he could but it was no use. Brer Fox had him firmly by the neck and held him right down to the ground.

"Let go, Brer Fox," he screamed. "Let me go or Brer Rabbit will escape. You've nearly got him, you're getting so close to him— just a few more chops and you'll have him."

"I'm a whole lot closer to you Brer Buzzard than I'll be to Brer Rabbit today," growled Brer Fox through a mouthful of feathers. "What did you want to trick me for?"

"Let me alone, Brer Fox," pleaded Brer Buzzard. "My old woman's waiting for me at home. Brer Rabbit's in there, I tell you."

"There's a bunch of his fur on that blackberry bush," said Brer Fox, "and that's not the way he came."

Then Brer Buzzard told Brer Fox what had really happened. "That Brer Rabbit is just about the lowest, no-good animal it's ever been my misfortune to come across," he said.

"That's neither here nor there, Brer Buzzard," said Brer Fox. "I left you to watch this hole and I left Brer Rabbit inside it. I come back and find you still at the hole right enough, but with no Brer Rabbit to be seen. I've had just about enough of all you creatures thinking you can do whatever you like with me. I'm going to throw you on the fire and burn you up. That's my last word."

"If you throw me on the fire, Brer Fox, it's only fair to warn you that I'll fly away," said Brer Buzzard.

"Well then, I'll deal with you right now," said Brer Fox.

Letting go of Brer Buzzard's neck he made a grab for his tail so that he could dash his head against the ground. Brer Buzzard's tail feathers came loose in a great bunch and he sailed up in the air like a rocket. As he flew up to a safe distance he screeched: "You gave me a good start, Brer Fox. Thanks a lot."

Poor old Brer Fox could do nothing but sit and watch him fly out of sight.

Brer Fox's new roof

One year Brer Rabbit built a new room at the side of his house. Of course everyone else immediately wanted to improve their own houses too: some built new extensions, some dug out cellars, some put in new windows, others simply made new curtains. Brer Fox decided to retile his roof.

As soon as Brer Rabbit heard about this he called round to see how the work was getting on. As he came near the house he heard a hammering noise, then caught sight of Brer Fox perched on top of the house, nailing tiles to the roof as fast as he could.

He saw something else as well. Hidden under the garden hedge was Brer Fox's lunch box. It was so bulging with food that the lid did not fit properly and it looked so appetizing that Brer Rabbit's stomach rumbled in anticipation.

"I'll eat that lunch or my name's not Brer Rabbit," he said to himself. Then he went up to the house and shouted up to Brer Fox.

"How is it coming on, Brer Fox?"

"Not now, Brer Rabbit, not now. I'm much too busy to waste time talking today," answered Brer Fox.

"What are you doing, then, Brer Fox?" said Brer Rabbit.

"What does it look like?" said Brer Fox crossly. "I'm retiling the roof before the wet season starts."

"Ah," said Brer Rabbit. Then, annoyingly, "What time is it, Brer Fox?"

"Time to work as far as I'm concerned," snapped Brer Fox.

Brer Rabbit stood looking at him for a moment. "Looks as if you could do with an extra pair of hands, Brer Fox," he said.

"Too true," said Brer Fox, balancing three tiles in one hand, a hammer in the other and holding half a dozen nails between his teeth. "But it doesn't look like my lucky day."

Brer Rabbit pulled his whiskers. "What about me, Brer Fox? I've been a very handy man with a hammer in my time."

"Why thank you, Brer Rabbit. That's a very kind offer."

Two seconds later Brer Rabbit was bounding up the ladder and had set to work. He managed to hang more tiles in one hour than Brer Fox had in two. Brer Rabbit really worked and worked but he was getting more tired and more hungry every minute. To make matters worse, Brer Fox was working above him on the roof and his long bushy tail kept getting in Brer Rabbit's way. Every time he pushed it aside the tail swung persistently back to where it had been before. Suddenly Brer Rabbit had an idea. He would cause a little accident.

Just as Brer Fox reached the top of the roof Brer Rabbit reached up and hammered a nail right through Brer Fox's tail and fixed it firmly to the ridge. Brer Fox could not move.

"Now look what you've done. You've nailed my tail to the roof."

Brer Rabbit mopped his forehead. "Don't be ridiculous. I couldn't have done a thing like that. No nail would go through that stupid thick tail of yours."

Brer Fox suddenly realized that his tail hurt and he screamed and kicked wildly. "You have nailed it, Brer Rabbit. For heaven's sake take that nail out."

But Brer Rabbit wasn't listening anymore. As soon as he saw that Brer Fox was firmly fixed he made straight for the ladder and started to climb down.

"To make out I hammer so badly I could nail your tail like that, Brer Fox. There's gratitude for you," he muttered crossly. "If I hadn't heard it myself I'd never have believed it."

"Oooouch," cried Brer Fox, struggling harder than ever.

"The very thought of how painful it would be makes me feel empty inside," said Brer Rabbit, reaching the ground. "Empty with horror, that's what I am. But if I'm not mistaken there's a box full of food over there that will just about fill me up."

Brer Fox's lunch was delicious and for almost five minutes Brer Rabbit was silent except for sounds of satisfied chewing. As he wiped his mouth with his sleeve he looked up at the now furious Brer Fox.

"Looks as if your tail is really stuck, Brer Fox. And I really am sorry for it. I must have been thinking about something else when I did that."

After that he just hopped out of the garden and went off to pester another neighbor, leaving someone else to take pity on Brer Fox and his long bushy tail.

Brer Fox sets a trap

For a long time after Brer Rabbit tricked Brer Fox, Brer Fox felt very bad. He felt angry and because he could not think what to do, he became very downhearted. One day as he was loping along the road with his tail between his legs, he met Brer Wolf. When they had finished saying good morning and asking after their families, Brer Wolf said:

"Is something wrong, Brer Fox? You haven't been your usual cunning self lately."

"Of course there's nothing wrong, Brer Wolf," said Brer Fox, forcing himself to laugh.

But Brer Wolf had a big, wise head and he decided to bring up the subject of Brer Rabbit later on, for the way Brer Rabbit had deceived Brer Fox was the talk of all the neighborhood. So Brer Wolf and Brer Fox chatted about this and that and then Brer Wolf mentioned casually that he had a plan to fix a trap for Brer Rabbit.

"How?" said Brer Fox very quickly.

"Get him inside your house," said Brer Wolf, "the rest is easy."

"The question is how are you going to get him there," said Brer Fox, beginning to lose interest.

"Trick him there," said Brer Wolf.

"Who's going to do the tricking?" said Brer Fox.

"I'll do the tricking if you'll do the catching," said Brer Wolf.

"How are you going to do it?"

"Like this," said Brer Wolf. "Run along home, go straight to bed and lie there pretending to be dead. Don't you say anything until Brer Rabbit comes right up close and puts his paws on you. And if we don't get him for supper this time . . ."

All this sounded like a good game and Brer Fox agreed. So he ambled off home while Brer Wolf made his way to Brer Rabbit's house.

When he got there it looked as if no one was at home but Brer Wolf walked up to the door and knocked—*blam blam!* Nobody came, so he knocked again—*blim blim!*

"Who's there?" asked Brer Rabbit.

"A friend," said Brer Wolf.

"Too many friends spoil the dinner," said Brer Rabbit. "Which friend might you be?"

"I bring bad news, Brer Rabbit," said Brer Wolf.

By this time Brer Rabbit had come to the door with his head tied up in a red handkerchief as if he had a bad toothache.

"Let's get it over with then," he said.

"Brer Fox died this morning," said Brer Wolf sadly. "I went down to his house a few minutes ago and there he was, lying stiff as a stick." With a deep, sad sigh Brer Wolf turned away and loped off. Brer Rabbit sat down and scratched his head and thought.

"Perhaps I'll just go down to Brer Fox's house and see if it's true," he said. And up he jumped and out he went.

When Brer Rabbit came close to Brer Fox's house it all looked quite deserted. He went nearer. Nothing stirred. He crept to the door, opened it quietly, and peered round the edge. There was Brer Fox, stretched out on the bed as large as life. Brer Rabbit pretended he was talking to himself.

"How sad," he said out loud. "Nobody's here to look after Brer Fox—not even Brer Buzzard has bothered to come to the funeral. I hope Brer Fox isn't dead but I suppose he is. Well, it's one way of finding out who your friends are. Even that Brer Wolf has gone off and left him. It's a really busy time of year for me too, but I'll stay here and watch over him." He paused and came a little nearer.

"He certainly looks dead but he might not be after all," he went on. "There's only one way I know of making sure. Whenever a visitor comes to say good-bye to the dead, the one who has died always waves his back leg and shouts 'Wahoo'!"

Brer Fox lay still. Then Brer Rabbit came even closer and spoke a little louder: "It's mighty funny. Brer Fox looks dead but he doesn't act dead. Dead folks always wave their back legs and shout 'Wahoo' when live folks come to see them. It's the only way you can be certain."

This was too much for Brer Fox. He shook his back leg and gave a deathly yell: *Wahoo!* And Brer Rabbit tore out of the house as if the dogs were after him.

Mr. Ram has visitors

Mr. Benjamin Ram looked very fierce to anyone who did not know him. His shaggy hair hung down around his neck and his curly horns looked sharp and dangerous. When he shook his head and snorted it seemed as if he made the earth shake.

Brer Fox was quite frightened of Mr. Ram. He chased his lambs when he had the chance but he never dared to go anywhere near Mr. Ram himself.

One day Brer Fox and Brer Wolf were walking along the road together discussing this and that. It was getting towards dinner time and Brer Fox was beginning to feel hungry.

"No need to feel hungry, Brer Fox," said Brer Wolf, "when we are right in Mr. Ram's neighborhood."

"Well," said Brer Fox doubtfully, "I'm not sure. He looks dangerous to me."

Brer Wolf roared with laughter. "Mr. Benjamin Ram dangerous? Why he never hurt a flea in his life. What kind of a fox are you anyway?"

Brer Fox gave Brer Wolf a hard look.

"I've seen you hungry many times in this district—and I've never heard you talking about making a meal out of Mr. Ram."

"I'm not frightened of Mr. Ram" said Brer Wolf. "I just don't like tough meat."

Brer Fox laughed. "You can't fool me, Brer Wolf. But instead of arguing with you I'm going to do what you suggest. I'm going to get old Mr. Benjamin Ram and I hope you'll be good enough to come with me. Just for the company, of course. I can manage the rest myself thank you."

Brer Wolf's jaw dropped open. "I'd rather go by myself," he said.

"All right, then," said Brer Fox. "Off you go. But you'd better hurry, because it isn't going to take me long to make mincemeat out of old Benjamin Ram."

Brer Wolf knew he could not back out now, so reluctantly he set off for Mr. Ram's

house in the forest, with Brer Fox trotting along behind laughing as Brer Wolf jumped nervously at every puff of wind.

Brer Wolf knocked on Mr. Ram's door and stood waiting for someone to open it. To his surprise, instead of opening the door, Mr. Ram came charging round the corner of the house and stood there with his red eyes gleaming and his shaggy hair blowing in the breeze. Brer Wolf's courage deserted him and he turned tail and fled back to where Brer Fox was standing waiting for him.

"Well," said Brer Fox mockingly, "had your dinner already, have you? Did you leave any for me?"

Brer Wolf looked glum. "I'm not feeling very well today," he grumbled. "And besides, I don't like old mutton."

"You may be sick in the stomach, but there's nothing much wrong with your legs, Brer Wolf. I just saw you use them."

"I was only running to see if it would

make me feel better," said Brer Wolf.

"I just want to lie down and be left alone when I'm feeling sick," said Brer Fox. "Still, everyone's different. I tell you what, I'll come and help you catch Mr. Ram."

"I know you, Brer Fox," said Brer Wolf. "You'll just run away and leave me to do all the dirty work."

"How can you say that, Brer Wolf? Look, to prove how wrong you are, I'll tie myself to you with this piece of rope."

So Brer Fox and Brer Wolf turned back together for Mr. Ram's house, securely tied to each other. Brer Wolf tended to hang back a little but he was too ashamed to say he was frightened and in any case, Brer Fox kept jerking the rope tight. When they came to the house, there was Mr. Ram, sitting on the porch sunning himself. As soon as he saw them coming he cleared his throat noisily and shouted:

"Brer Fox, thank you so much for catching that villain and bringing him back

here. There's not much food about these days. My storehouse is quite empty."

Just then Mrs. Ram saw Brer Fox and Brer Wolf through the window and she bleated so loudly you could hear her right down in the village. Mr. Ram wasn't feeling too brave himself by this time but he kept on talking:

"Bring him in, now, Brer Fox. Can't you hear the old woman asking for him? She hasn't had wolf meat now for nearly a month, and it's a great favorite with her. Come on now, Brer Fox, bring him in."

Brer Wolf tried to untie himself but the knot was so tight that he decided simply to make a run for it. He broke away and ran, dragging Brer Fox along behind him as if he weighed no more than a feather. It was many a day before Brer Fox recovered from the thumps and bumps and scratches he received on his unexpected journey. And you can be sure that neither Brer Fox nor Brer Wolf went near Mr. Ram's place again.

Brer Rabbit's new shoes

One day Brer Rabbit had to go into the town to buy some extra winter supplies for his family.

"How can I go looking like this?" he said to his wife. "I've no shoes and no jacket. I'm ashamed to show my face in town."

"If you don't go we'll have no food to see us through the winter," said his wife.

So Brer Rabbit made himself look as smart as he could, took down his walking stick and set off for town. After a while he came to a place where some people had been camping the night before and as it was a cold morning he sat down to warm his feet by the hot ashes they had left.

As he was sitting there looking at his toes and feeling sorry for himself, he heard something trotting down the road. It was Mr. Dog, smelling and sniffling around to see if there were any scraps left by the fire. Mr. Dog was all dressed up in his best Sunday clothes. And he was wearing a brand-new pair of shoes.

When Brer Rabbit saw the shoes he felt very bad but he managed to hide his feelings. He bowed politely to Mr. Dog and Mr. Dog bowed politely to him.

"Good morning, Mr. Dog," said Brer Rabbit. "And where are you going in all those fine clothes?"

"I'm going to town, Brer Rabbit. Where are you off to?"

"I thought I'd go to town myself and buy a new pair of shoes. My old ones are worn out and they hurt my feet so badly I can't wear them anymore. Those are very nice shoes you are wearing, Mr. Dog. Where did you get them?"

"Down in town, Brer Rabbit, down in town," said Mr. Dog.

"They fit you very well, Mr. Dog," said Brer Rabbit. "I wonder, would you be so good as to let me try one of them on? Then I'll know what size to ask for in the shop."

"Certainly, Brer Rabbit," said Mr. Dog

and he sat on a fallen log and took off one of the shoes. Brer Rabbit put it on and trotted off down the road for a short distance. Then he came back, limping slightly.

"That shoe fits me really well, Mr. Dog," he said. "But it's difficult to tell with just one shoe. It makes me trot lop-sidedly."

"Why don't you try them both?" asked Mr. Dog, pulling off the other shoe. Brer Rabbit put on the second shoe and trotted off down the road.

"Why they are just right for me," he said as he came back. "I'll certainly try to get some like these. There's just one other thing you can help me with if you will. That jacket of yours. I'm hoping to buy one for myself today and I really don't know what style is best. If I try yours on perhaps it will help me to make up my mind."

"Go ahead," said Mr. Dog, taking off the

jacket and handing it over to Brer Rabbit.

"I'll just walk up the road a bit and get the feel of it," said Brer Rabbit, and he set off once more. But this time, when he came to the spot where he had turned round before, he laid his ears back and ran as fast as he could for the woods.

"Hey," called Mr. Dog. "What do you think you're doing?"

Brer Rabbit went on running.

"Hey, come back!"

Mr. Dog set off after Brer Rabbit, but he was too far behind and, in a few minutes, Brer Rabbit had vanished into the tangled undergrowth in the woods.

Mr. Dog kept on running here and there through the woods, barking and sniffing and scratching at the ground with his paws whenever he thought he saw a rabbit hole. It was no use. Brer Rabbit—and the shoes and the fine new jacket—had disappeared.

From that day to this, Mr. Dog and Brer Rabbit have never been friends. Mr. Dog chases Brer Rabbit whenever he sees or smells him and Brer Rabbit takes care to keep well out of his way.

Brer Wolf says grace

One day Brer Rabbit was returning from visiting some old friends of his when he came across a large basket lying by the side of the road.

"Hello," said Brer Rabbit to himself. "What's this?"

He looked up and down the road but saw no one. He listened and listened but heard nothing. He waited and waited but nobody came.

"Must have fallen off the back of a wagon," said Brer Rabbit. "I'd better look inside to make sure it isn't damaged at all."

Then Brer Rabbit lifted the lid of the basket and peeped into it. It seemed to be half-full of fresh, juicy lettuces. He put his hand in and pulled one out. Then, "It looks like lettuce," he muttered. He pulled a few leaves off. "And it feels like lettuce." He began to nibble a leaf thoughtfully. "And it tastes like lettuce. In fact it tastes like the best lettuce I've eaten this year."

Then he jumped into the basket, landing right in the middle of the pile of soft green leaves and began to munch greedily.

33

To Brer Rabbit's surprise the pile of lettuces gave a deep growl—*grrrr*—and before he could leap out again Brer Wolf uncoiled his long body from the bottom of the basket and grabbed him with both his front paws.

Brer Rabbit hated to be outwitted.

"Ha ha," he laughed nervously. "I was just trying to frighten you, Brer Wolf. Of course I knew you were in there because I could smell you. There's no mistaking the smell of wolf, you know."

"I'm so glad you recognized me," growled Brer Wolf, "because I recognized you the minute you dropped in on me. In fact I was expecting you. Why, I said to Brer Fox just yesterday that I was going to have a nap in this basket and I was sure you would come along and wake me up. And sure enough you did."

Brer Rabbit began to be very frightened as he realized he had fallen into a well-prepared trap.

"Oh please let me go, Brer Wolf," he pleaded.

Brer Wolf just grinned more wolfishly than ever and, giving Brer Rabbit's head a sharp jerk, he began to drag him out of the basket.

"Where are you taking me, Brer Wolf?" asked Brer Rabbit.

"Down to the spring, Brer Rabbit," said Brer Wolf.

"What for?" asked Brer Rabbit timidly.

"So I can wash you before I skin you," said Brer Wolf.

"Please sir, please let me go," begged Brer Rabbit, really frightened now by Brer Wolf's determined look.

"You'll be lucky," said Brer Wolf.

"But Brer Wolf, all that lettuce has made me feel so ill."

"You'll feel worse before I've finished with you."

"But where I come from it's not considered polite to eat people who feel sick," said Brer Rabbit.

"I'm afraid that where I come from, it's not considered good manners to eat any other sort," replied Brer Wolf.

This went on until they reached the spring. Brer Rabbit begged and pleaded and pleaded and begged. Brer Wolf just grinned and grinned. Eventually, Brer Wolf dropped Brer Rabbit on the ground and held him down with his front paws while he

considered how to deal with him. Meanwhile, Brer Rabbit was doing some considering of his own. Just when it looked as if Brer Wolf was ready to act, Brer Rabbit burst into tears:

"B-B-B-Brer W-W-W-Wolf, are you really going to sacrifice me now?" he sobbed.

"That I am, Brer Rabbit, that I am."

"Well if I really have to die, B-B-Brer W-W-Wolf, please make sure you kill me decently. And if I really have to be eaten, please eat me decently too."

"What do you mean, Brer Rabbit?" asked Brer Wolf crossly.

"Just be as polite as you can possibly be, Brer Wolf. Please say grace first, and please say it quickly because I'm getting very weak."

"How do I say grace, Brer Rabbit?" asked Brer Wolf, thinking this was a particularly strange request.

"Just put your front paws under your chin," said Brer Rabbit, "shut your eyes and say 'For what we are about to receive . . .' and please say it quickly, Brer Wolf, because I am getting weaker and weaker."

Brer Wolf dutifully held his front paws under his chin, closed his eyes and began to say "For what . . ." He got no further. As soon as he let go of Brer Rabbit, Brer Rabbit was off like greased lightning and all Brer Wolf could see was a white tail bobbing away into the distance. But it was a long time before Brer Rabbit really enjoyed a lettuce again.

Brer Fox's fish trap

One summer Brer Fox and Brer Rabbit went to live on the banks of the river. It was a very pleasant place to live and there were plenty of fresh green plants for Brer Rabbit to eat. Brer Fox did not do so well and after a time he began to long for the taste of fresh fish.

"Let's make a fish trap," he said one day to Brer Rabbit.

"Best of luck, Brer Fox," said Brer Rabbit. "But I'm not too fond of fish myself and I certainly haven't time to make a trap."

"Then I'll do it myself," said Brer Fox.

He spent several days drawing up elaborate plans and even longer finding the wood and fitting it all together. The next problem was where to put the trap but at last he found the place he wanted. Brer Rabbit sat on the bank watching and sunning himself as Brer Fox dragged stones and fixed the trap firmly in position. Then, exhausted, Brer Fox went home to rest.

After a while Brer Fox went down to see if any fish had entered the trap. He plunged his paw into the water, felt all round but there were no fish. He came back later in the day but there was still nothing there.

"Better wait until morning," he thought. But the morning was no better. Somehow or other the fish were avoiding the trap completely.

Brer Fox visited the trap three times a day for more than a week, all the time getting more and more desperate for some fresh fish. One morning he went there very early, just as it began to get light. Something about the trap looked different.

"Someone's been here before me," thought Brer Fox. "Someone's been robbing my trap all this time and I'm going to find out who that someone is."

Brer Fox climbed into his boat and paddled over to the other bank where some overhanging bushes hid him from view. He settled down to watch the trap.

Brer Fox watched all morning. Nobody came. He watched all afternoon. Nobody came. Night fell and he was just about to give up and go home when he heard a rustling sound on the other side of the river. Who should he see but Brer Rabbit, standing up in a little boat, poling it straight towards the fish trap.

"He can't even row a boat properly," muttered Brer Fox, who prided himself on his skill. "Fancy standing up like that at the back of the boat. I won't have much trouble catching *him*."

Brer Rabbit poled up to the fish trap, felt around inside it and pulled out a great big pike. Then he reached in and pulled out

another, then a perch, then a couple of trout. Before long he had a great heap of fish in the bottom of his boat.

Brer Fox took his oars and sped out from under the bushes.

"Hey, stop that. So you're the one that's been robbing my fish trap all this time are you? I've got you this time. And it's no use trying to get away either."

Quick as a flash, Brer Rabbit snatched up his pole and pushed off, with Brer Fox close behind. Now it is true that Brer Fox was a good oarsman but in this case he was in a difficult position. Because he was rowing a boat, Brer Fox had to sit with his back to the direction in which he was going, so he could not keep a close eye on Brer Rabbit. Brer Rabbit on the other hand was standing at the back of his boat—with a long pole in his hand. All he had to do when Brer Fox came too near was to push his pole against Brer Fox's boat and propel himself swiftly out of reach. The harder he pushed Brer Fox's boat back, the faster his own moved forwards and in no time at all Brer Rabbit, his boat and all the fish had vanished round a bend in the river.

Poor Brer Fox went without his dinner again.

Brer Rabbit spoils a party

One day Brer Fox decided to give a party. He invited Brer Bear, Brer Wolf and Brer Raccoon and many others but he decided he would not ask Brer Rabbit.

"Let's have a quiet, peaceful party for once," he said to his wife.

It was not easy to hide a party from Brer Rabbit and very soon he found out when and where it was to be held.

"I may not be invited," said Brer Rabbit, "but just you wait. I'll have more fun than the real guests."

The day of the party came and everyone who had been invited went to Brer Fox's house and began to eat and drink and enjoy themselves.

While they were busy talking and laughing, Brer Rabbit scurried about arranging his own plan. He had recently been to a barbecue where a band had played and while no one was looking he had managed to "borrow" one of the drums.

"You never know when it will come in useful," he said to his wife. Now he took the drum out of its hiding place and marched off down the road towards Brer Fox's house, beating it as hard as he could.

Diddydum, diddydum, diddydum-dum-dum —diddydum! went the drum.

At first the party guests were making such a noise themselves that they could not hear anything but Brer Rabbit came nearer, beating the drum until it sounded like thunder.

Diddydum, diddydum, diddydum-dum-dum —diddydum!

After a while, Brer Raccoon, who always kept one ear open for anything interesting that might be going on said:

"What's that noise, Brer Fox?"

Brer Fox stopped talking for a minute and went to the window to listen. The sound was coming nearer and nearer:

Diddydum-diddydum, diddydum-dum-dum —diddydum!

One by one the animals stopped talking and soon the booming sound of the drum filled the room.

"Soldiers," said Brer Fox.

"Bandits," said Brer Bear.

Brer Raccoon was the first to move. He reached under his chair for his hat and said: "I think I'd better be going now. I told my wife I'd only be gone for a few minutes and—er—she doesn't like me to be late."

Brer Raccoon hurried out but by the time he had reached the back gate all the others had caught up with him—including Brer Fox. Off they all went, scrambling over one another in the rush and not stopping for breath until they were safely in the bushes.

When Brer Rabbit arrived at the house, it was quite deserted. Brer Rabbit put his mouth to the drum air hole and, making a noise like a loud megaphone boomed:

"Is anybody there? No of course not," he replied for them. "They've all run off."

Brer Rabbit burst out laughing and marched defiantly into Brer Fox's living room. He wiped his feet on the new carpet, sat down on the best chair and put his feet up on the sofa.

"Might as well make myself comfortable," he said, reaching out for a tray of cookies and pouring himself a large drink.

"Can't let all this good food go to waste." And he helped himself to some more.

All this time the other animals were hiding in the thick bushes, listening for more strange sounds, ready to make a dash for it if they heard anything. But all was quiet and still.

"I'm going back," said Brer Fox at last. "I don't like to leave the house empty if something dangerous is around the place."

The others reluctantly agreed to go with him and they all crept cautiously back towards the house, freezing like statues if they heard a twig rustle.

The first thing they saw when they opened the door was Brer Rabbit, sprawled in a chair with his feet on the sofa, a glass in one hand and a half-eaten sandwich in the other. His head was lolling against the back of the chair, his eyes were closed and he was snoring gently. Cake crumbs and crushed nuts littered the carpet around his feet.

Brer Fox stood and looked at him for a moment. Then he put his mouth close to one of Brer Rabbit's ears: "You've made fun of me once too often, Brer Rabbit. But I've got you this time." The others clustered round. "WAKE UP," shouted Brer Fox at the top of his voice.

Brer Rabbit woke with a start and took in the situation immediately. There was Brer Fox leering right into his face, his teeth looking particularly fierce. And there were all the other animals, laughing at him unkindly. Brer Rabbit pretended to be dazed with food and sleep. He jumped to his feet and began staggering round the room like a seasick rabbit in a storm, hitting out at everything and anything with his fists, and rolling his eyes as if he were still in the middle of a nightmare.

"Put your hands up and fight, you cowards. Just give me a little room and come at me one at a time and I'll soon show you a fight. Come on and fight now."

Brer Fox stepped forwards and grabbed Brer Rabbit by the arm.

"Wake up and stop clowning around," he said. "This time I mean business. Now, Brer Bear. You've a reputation for being a fair-minded man. What do you think should be done with someone like this rabbit?"

Brer Bear had been sniggering with the other guests at Brer Rabbit's antics. Now he put on his spectacles, looked very solemn, cleared his throat and said: "This is a serious matter and no mistake. This creature has not only shattered our quiet afternoon with his ear-splitting noise. He has not only run us out of the house at considerable risk of shock to some of us older ones. On top of this he has forced his way in (quite uninvited) and helped himself to as much free food and drink as he wanted. There's only one thing good enough for a villain like this. Throw him in the water."

"Oh please, Brer Bear," said Brer Rabbit in a pleading voice. "Show me some kindness. Don't throw me into the stream. The current runs so fast there and I'll break my neck on the sharp rocks. Throw me in the deep river where at least I'll have a chance to swim."

"Why didn't I think of that?" said Brer Fox. "The stream is just the place."

Brer Rabbit pretended to be more worried than he really was.

"Well if you must throw me in, then just grant me one last request. Spare me a walking stick so I have something to hold on-to while I'm drowning."

Brer Bear scratched his head.

"As far as I remember there's nothing in the law that says a drowning man can't have a walking stick," he said wisely.

Brer Fox fetched a walking stick from the corner by the door and the animals bundled Brer Rabbit into a wheelbarrow and bumped and thumped him to the bank of the stream.

With a heave and a shout they tipped him over the edge into the water.

Brer Rabbit landed lightly on all fours, just like a cat, but in an instant he was on his feet in the shallow water, which hardly came up to his ankles. Using the cane to help him, he picked his way over the stones to the other side of the stream.

"So long, Brer Fox. Thanks for the nice party," he laughed, disappearing as fast as he could into the bushes.

Brer Rabbit opens the bag

One day Brer Fox was sauntering down the road when he noticed Brer Terrapin walking home rather wearily.

"Looks like a good time to catch the old nuisance," thought Brer Fox and he ran back to his house and picked up a small bag. A few minutes later he was creeping up behind Brer Terrapin and in no time at all he had scooped him up into the bag and slung it over his shoulder.

"Help!" shouted Brer Terrapin, struggling feebly. He kicked and scratched and tried to bite through the bag but it was useless.

It so happened that Brer Rabbit was sitting under the hedge by the road when Brer Fox passed by with what looked like a bag of jumping potatoes over his shoulder.

"Now what does he have in that bag?" said Brer Rabbit. "I wonder what it can be."

Brer Rabbit was a very inquisitive rabbit indeed and he could not bear not to know what was going on.

"Brer Fox has no right to carry a mystery bag like that around without telling folks what he's got in it," he said. "It's my duty as a good citizen to find out what's going on."

Brer Rabbit set off as fast as he could for Brer Fox's house, taking a shortcut by the watermelon patch (and even having time for a quick snack there). He arrived before Brer Fox and hid among the bushes by the door. After a while Brer Fox arrived, still with the bag on his shoulder. He opened the door and, dropping the bag in the corner, sat down to get his breath back. But Brer Rabbit did not give him a chance to settle down. Brer Fox had hardly loosened his jacket when Brer Rabbit's head appeared round the door, looking very worried indeed.

"Quick, Brer Fox. There's no time to sit around daydreaming. Get your stick and run down to the melon patch as fast as you can. I was there a moment ago and I saw a whole bunch of people trampling all over the melons, stealing the ones they weren't

eating there and then. I shouted at them to stop but I don't exactly look frightening and they took no notice at all. Hurry, Brer Fox, hurry. I'd come with you but I'm rushing home myself to my wife with some medicine. She's not at all well, you know."

Brer Rabbit disappeared and darted straight back to his hiding place in the bushes. Meanwhile Brer Fox grabbed his walking stick and marched off towards the melon patch looking like thunder. Brer Rabbit strolled confidently into the house, knowing he had plenty of time. He saw the bag at once and began to prod it and poke it to find out what it could be. Suddenly the bag shouted:

"That hurts. Go away, let me alone will you? Ouch."

Brer Rabbit was astonished. Then he began to laugh. "Is that you Brer Terrapin? It must be. Nobody else could make such a fuss."

"Hey, that's Brer Rabbit, isn't it?"

"It certainly is," said Brer Rabbit.

"Then get me out of here," squeaked Brer Terrapin. "I've flour in my throat and grit in my eyes and I can hardly breathe in here. Get me out."

Brer Terrapin's voice sounded muffled and far away. Brer Rabbit couldn't stop laughing.

"You really are a smart fellow, Brer

Terrapin," he snorted. "Much smarter than I am. I can see how you got in the bag—but I really can't understand how you managed to tie it up so well from inside. I just can't figure it out."

Brer Terrapin tried to explain but Brer Rabbit just laughed. At last he recovered enough to untie the bag and carry Brer Terrapin off to safety in the woods. Brer Rabbit had not finished with Brer Fox yet, however. While he was hustling Brer Terrapin to safety he saw a hornets' nest in the bottom of a hollow tree. He quickly covered the tiny hole where the hornets flew in and out with his hand and carried the nest carefully to Brer Fox's house. He slipped it into the bag, tied it up firmly and made sure there were no signs of any disturbance in the rest of the house. Then he picked up the bag and threw it against the floor, kicked it and flung it several times against the wall to make the hornets thoroughly angry. Replacing the bag carefully back in the corner where he had found it, he crept out to join Brer Terrapin and watch the fun.

They did not have long to wait. Brer Fox came striding back from the melon patch looking furious. He threw his walking stick on the ground and slammed the door shut behind him. Everything went quiet. Then suddenly the most amazing commotion broke out in the house. Brer Rabbit and Brer Terrapin agreed it sounded as if a herd of cows had stampeded into the room. Chairs were being hurled about, the table flew past the window upside down, pieces of crockery shattered noisily on the floor. With a mighty crash the front door flew off its hinges and Brer Fox ran outside waving his arms like a windmill, beating off an angry swarm of hornets as he ran. Brer Rabbit and Brer Terrapin watched in amazement as he zigzagged out of sight, making for the nearest pond. Then they both burst out laughing.

"That'll teach him to put things in bags that are better left alone," said Brer Terrapin between giggles.

Brer Rabbit gets a fright

One day Mr. Wildcat was lying stretched out taking his afternoon nap on the branch of a tree which hung low over the road. He was just beginning to wake up when who should he see loping along the road below but Brer Rabbit.

"Aha," purred Mr. Wildcat. "Just what I've been waiting for!"

Lippity clippity, clippity lippity, Brer Rabbit hopped nearer and nearer, without a care in the world. Then—*clumpf.* All of a sudden something large and soft and furry fell right on top of him and pinned him firmly to the ground.

"Ouf," said Brer Rabbit, struggling for breath, then, "Ow, that hurts," as he felt Mr. Wildcat's claws digging into his back. "Now what have I done?"

Mr. Wildcat stood up and, still holding on to Brer Rabbit, rubbed his wet nose on Brer Rabbit's ear and whispered menacingly:

"I'm so fond of you, Brer Rabbit." He purred and a shiver ran up Brer Rabbit's spine. "I'm just so fond of you that I can't let you go." Then he growled fiercely. "What have you done, Brer Rabbit? Why, you've been fooling all my friends and relations—and you've even set my cousin Fox on me. To be quite honest I've had enough." He laughed and ground his teeth right next to Brer Rabbit's ear.

Brer Rabbit's own teeth chattered but he managed to stammer: "Whatever I might have done to your relations, I've never done you any harm, have I, Mr. Wildcat?"

"No, Brer Rabbit, I can't say you have," said Mr. Wildcat thoughtfully.

"What's more, I've always done my best to do you good turns. And even though you are gripping my fur in that very unfriendly way I'm willing to do you yet another good turn."

"Mmmmm?" purred Mr. Wildcat, still sounding very sinister.

"I heard some wild turkeys back down

46

"Joking, Mr. Wildcat? At a time like this? It's hardly the time to make jokes."

Gradually Mr. Wildcat was convinced that Brer Rabbit was telling the truth so he lay down on the road and looked as dead as he possibly could.

Meanwhile Brer Rabbit made off down the road to fetch the turkeys. Brer Rabbit was very persuasive and it wasn't long before the turkeys were parading along the road, led by old Brer Gibbley Gobbler. Mr. Wildcat lay still, thinking about the feast of turkey meat that was on its way.

Just as the crowd of turkeys drew near, Brer Rabbit whispered to Brer Gibbley Gobbler that it was a trap. By the time they came to where Mr. Wildcat was lying the whole turkey family was arguing tooth and nail about whether Mr. Wildcat was really dead or not. They argued as loudly as possible to make quite sure that Mr. Wildcat knew what was going on.

Mr. Wildcat lay there, motionless. The wind ruffled his hair and the sun shone down on him but still he didn't move. The turkeys clucked but did not get too close. They shouted and argued—but they kept a safe distance. Eventually Mr. Wildcat grew tired of waiting. He jumped up and made a grab for the nearest turkey. The turkey was ready for him. Just as Mr. Wildcat's claws were about to grab him, he flew up into the air—and Mr. Wildcat ran right under him. He ran at another one, but that turkey flew off too, and so did another and another one until Mr. Wildcat was so short of breath that he just had to lie down on the ground again to rest.

Realizing they were safe, old Brer Gibbley Gobbler and his family turned and paraded back down the road the way they had come, still arguing and quarrelling about the trap. From that day on, turkeys have never stopped arguing. If you meet a turkey yourself and start arguing you can be pretty sure it will begin arguing right back at you.

Not surprisingly, in the middle of all this fuss and noise, Brer Rabbit had made quite sure he was nowhere to be seen.

the road and if you'd be so kind as to let me go for a minute I'll go and call them. You can play dead in the middle of the road and when they come up to you, all you have to do is jump up and take your pick of the best of them."

Mr. Wildcat looked thoughtful. If there was one kind of meat he liked it was wild turkey meat.

"You're quite sure you're not joking, Brer Rabbit?"

Miss Goose catches a burglar

One day Brer Fox and Brer Rabbit were sitting around the cotton patch. Brer Fox was on one side of the fence and Brer Rabbit on the other—at a safe distance. They were arguing as usual when suddenly they heard a strange sound—*blim, blim, blim.*

"What's all that noise about?" demanded Brer Fox.

"That'll be old Miss Goose down at the spring doing her washing."

"All by herself is she?" asked Brer Fox.

"I expect so," said Brer Rabbit. "It's best to keep out of the way when old Miss Goose is doing her spring cleaning."

Brer Fox looked crafty. "Maybe I'll just wander on down and say good morning," he muttered to himself. But what he was really thinking of was a fat, tasty goose for supper.

Brer Rabbit's sharp ears picked up Brer Fox's words and his sharp brain immediately suspected what was in Brer Fox's mind.

"Well, I'll be off home now," said Brer Fox loudly. "See you tomorrow."

"See you tomorrow," said Brer Rabbit. "If not before," he added, chuckling to himself under his breath.

Brer Fox set off towards his home but Brer Rabbit, keeping well out of sight, hopped round to see Miss Goose. There she was, down by the spring, busy washing and scrubbing and beating the clothes.

"Morning, Miss Goose," said Brer Rabbit.

"Morning, Brer Rabbit," said Miss Goose. "I'm sorry I can't shake hands with you but I'm all covered in soap."

"Don't you worry about that, Miss Goose," said Brer Rabbit. "I know your heart's in the right place."

"I should hope so, Brer Rabbit," said Miss Goose, "but to tell you the truth I sometimes wonder. I'm that full of aches and pains these days. I'm growing stiff and I'm growing clumsy. What's worse, I'm losing my sight. Just before you came along

49

I dropped my spectacles in the tub and if you'd come along then I'd have taken you for that nasty Brer Fox. Goodness knows what I might have done then—poured boiling water over your head I should think. I don't know what I'd do without my spectacles."

"Talking about Brer Fox," said Brer Rabbit, "it wouldn't surprise me if he wasn't planning to pay you a visit."

Miss Goose let out an agitated cackle. She wiped her wings on her apron, pushed her spectacles up onto her forehead and looked extremely worried.

"You're not fooling me, Brer Rabbit? Oh dear, oh dear, suppose he really does come? What am I going to do? There isn't even a Mr. Goose about the house to protect me."

"Well now, Miss Goose—you look as though you've been a high flier in your time and even though you look a bit, well, older now, if you don't fly high tonight you might as well give up here and now. Listen and I'll tell you exactly what to do."

That evening, Miss Goose made up a large bundle of clean white sheets and laid it on her bed in the far corner of the room. Turning out the lights, she flew heavily up onto the rafter that ran across the ceiling and perched securely out of reach. By the back door lay another surprise, Mr. Dog, a big, well-trained farm dog who had agreed to stay—just in case anything happened.

Sure enough, just before dawn, Brer Fox's long, stealthy body crept along the garden fence, slunk under the gate and up the path to the front door. He gave the door a gentle push and disappeared silently inside.

The white bundle on the bed gleamed faintly in the dark room and, certain that there lay Miss Goose, Brer Fox leaped onto it and began to drag it towards the door. But Miss Goose was not on the bed.

"You thieving, murdering, good-for-nothing fox," she screeched from above Brer Fox's head. "What do you think you've got there? Just you leave my clean washing alone, you filthy animal."

Brer Fox dropped the bundle in surprise —and just in time. A snarling, angry Mr.

Dog was advancing towards him from the back door. Without waiting for a second look, Brer Fox sprinted for the door and was out and away in no time at all.

Where do you think Brer Rabbit was all this time? Why he was safely tucked up in bed. But he had not finished with Brer Fox. Somehow or other a rumor started in the neighborhood that Brer Fox had tried and failed to steal Miss Goose's best clothes, a rumor that quite ruined Brer Fox's reputation as a proud, cunning operator. Even today Brer Fox still thinks it was Brer Rabbit who persuaded Mr. Dog to lie in wait for him—and Brer Rabbit is happy to let him think so. And the bad feeling between foxes and dogs also started that night at Miss Goose's house. Nowadays they will fight as soon as look at one another.

50

Brer Rabbit's luck runs out

In the days when Brer Rabbit was annoying everyone with his spiteful tricks, the other animals spent a great deal of time discussing how to catch him at it. They discussed it while they worked; they discussed it in the evenings round the fire; they nearly wore themselves out discussing it. After a while it became clear that no ordinary plans and traps would catch Brer Rabbit—he was far too cunning for that. The only thing that might work was magic.

"If you ask me, Brer Rabbit is a witch himself," said Brer Bear.

"If not, he's certainly working closely with one."

"I think he's just lucky," said Brer Fox. "But why is all the luck on his side? It's uncanny."

The more they thought about this the stranger it seemed and in the end—after days and nights of argument—they worked out a scheme to discover Brer Rabbit's secret.

One day Mrs. Rabbit was sitting at home when Brer Bear came panting in.

"Mrs. Rabbit," he said, "you know all about children's illnesses. Would you mind coming to have a look at my young Klibs? My wife's been up half the night with him."

"Of course, Brer Bear," said Mrs. Rabbit, and, making sure that her own little rabbits were safe, she collected her bag of herbs and medicines and set out.

At Brer Bear's house she found Mrs. Bear sitting by the fire nursing Klibs, with all the wives of the neighborhood whispering and gossiping around her.

"Come right in," said Mrs. Bear, "I'm so pleased to see you. I hope you've brought your knitting with you because I'm very bad company when one of the kids is sick. Just throw your coat on the bed there. Mrs. Wolf, give Mrs. Rabbit the rocking chair. It's a long way from her house to mine. When he wakes up perhaps you'd have a look at Klibs would you? I don't want to disturb him now he's asleep at last."

Mrs. Bear chatted on in a friendly way about this and that and Mrs. Rabbit sat down, took out her knitting and settled in for a comfortable day.

All this time Brer Wolf was sitting on the back porch in his old chair, dozing in the sun. Before long there was a lull in the conversation and Mrs. Rabbit began to think about her own business. Suddenly she threw her knitting on the floor and stood up with a gasp.

"Goodness gracious. Do you know what I've done? I've come away and left my old man's money purse lying on the mantelshelf. Oh dear. It's not the money—there's little enough of that in it—but there's something else inside that Brer Rabbit values more than anything. Oh I'm so forgetful these days I don't know what to do."

Brer Wolf pricked up his ears and opened one eye. Mrs. Bear (who knew all about the plan, of course) jolted young Klibs so clumsily from one knee to the other that she very nearly dropped him.

"Rather you than me, Mrs. Rabbit. If I'd left Mr. Bear's money lying around like that he'd just about tear the place to bits. But don't you worry. I'm sure it will be quite safe. Ah, look now, Klibs is waking up. Perhaps you'd have a look at him now."

Meanwhile Mr. Wolf very quietly crept out of the back gate and made off for Brer Rabbit's house. Brer Wolf could run like a racehorse when he felt like it and very soon he was opening the door. The little rabbits were tucked up fast asleep having their afternoon nap. One of them stirred as the door creaked.

"Is that you Mommy?"

"Sh—sh. Go to sleep, honey, or the big bad wolf will get you," whispered Brer Wolf in a rabbity voice. The little rabbit began to whimper but in a few minutes he had whimpered himself back to sleep.

Brer Wolf waited until he was quite sure they were all safely sleeping again. Then he tiptoed to the mantelshelf and felt all along it, picking up the ornaments and almost knocking the clock off in his haste. At last he found what he was looking for. With Brer Rabbit's money purse clasped firmly in his hand he ran off as fast as he could.

When he was out of sight of the house Brer Wolf sat down to examine the treasure. It was one of those purses that are divided into two parts. In one half Brer Wolf found a few small coins but in the other he discovered what he was looking for: a large

lucky charm in the shape of a rabbit's foot.

"Aha," cried Brer Wolf, bounding off for home as pleased as if he'd found a gold mine.

Brer Rabbit did not miss his lucky rabbit's foot for some time but when he did notice it was gone he really missed it badly. He worried so much about it that he made himself quite ill.

"I know I left it there," he said over and over again. "But if I left it there where is it?"

Mrs. Rabbit said nothing.

While Brer Rabbit moped around, Brer Wolf was quite the opposite. It looked as if he now had all the luck that Brer Rabbit had lost. Brer Wolf grew fatter as Brer Rabbit grew thinner; Brer Wolf ran and jumped about the place while Brer Rabbit plodded along as heavily as Sister Cow; Brer Wolf's garden produced pounds of juicy carrots and cabbages while Brer Rabbit's could only raise a few pale lettuces half-eaten away by caterpillars.

"There's only one thing for it," said Brer Rabbit to his wife. "I'll have to go on a journey to consult Mammy-Bammy Big-Money."

Mammy-Bammy Big-Money was a witch-rabbit. She lived far out in the deep, dark swamp and to get to her home involved a long and complicated journey. Only the very bravest and most determined animals managed to reach her. It took Brer Rabbit several days to get there even though he knew the way and by the time he arrived he was quite worn out.

No one had ever actually seen Mammy-Bammy Big-Money. She lived in a hole in the ground on an island surrounded by dark, shallow water. A leaky row boat carried visitors to her lair. At first the only sound that Brer Rabbit could hear was the noise of croaking frogs and the dripping of water from the overhanging trees. Then even the frogs were silent. A plume of black smoke began to rise from the witch-rabbit's hole. The smoke became blacker and blacker and when it was as thick and as dark as it could possibly be, Brer Rabbit knew it was time to speak.

"Mammy-Bammy Big-Money," he said in a shrill, frightened voice. "I need your **help, Mammy**."

"Son Riley Rabbit, why so?" came a voice from deep underground. "Son Riley Rabbit, why so?"

"Mammy, I lost the rabbit's foot you gave me."

"Oh Riley Rabbit, why so?"

"Mammy, I put it down and I don't know where I left it. My luck has run right off with the foot."

There was a pause as smoke continued to stream out of the burrow. Then: "The wolf stole your good luck, Son Riley Rabbit. He has it now. He carries it always next to his heart. Wait and you will find your luck again."

There was a gulping sound as Mammy-Bammy Big-Money sucked all the black smoke back into the hole. Then the swamp was silent again. After what seemed like hours the frogs began to croak again and Brer Rabbit set off for home.

Brer Rabbit did not act at once after he returned from his strange visit. In fact he tried to behave as if nothing had happened. But all the time he was waiting and watching, watching and waiting, hanging around Brer Wolf's house and getting to know all his movements. One day he heard that Brer Wolf was invited to a big wedding in the next village.

"Now's my chance," said Brer Rabbit— but he still kept his eyes and ears open and he still pretended to look miserable.

The morning after the wedding, Brer Rabbit watched Brer Wolf come out of the house and go down to the spring for a bucket of water. He slipped up to the door and peered in. Mrs. Wolf was busy frying meat for breakfast and there, hanging carelessly over the back of the chair, was Brer Wolf's best jacket. Brer Rabbit could just see the tip of his money purse poking out of the top pocket. Brer Rabbit rattled the door handle noisily and rushed in, panting as if he had been running fast.

"Good morning, Mrs. Wolf. I met Brer Wolf down at the spring and he sent me back for his shaving brush. He says he keeps it in that old money purse I lent him."

"Dear me, Brer Rabbit, how you frightened me," said Mrs. Wolf, almost dropping the frying pan. The words were hardly out of her mouth when Brer Rabbit darted over to the chair, snatched the money purse out of Brer Wolf's jacket pocket and vanished down the road, clutching his precious rabbit's foot.

And after that you can be sure Brer Rabbit's luck was just as good as ever.

Brer Rabbit goes milking

One day Brer Rabbit was loping along home after a long day in the sun. He felt very tired and hungry. He was very thirsty, too, and when he saw Sister Cow grazing in her field he made up his mind to get some of her milk to drink.

Brer Rabbit knew very well that Sister Cow would not give him any milk willingly. She had refused him more than once— even when his wife was sick. But Brer Rabbit had a plan. He danced up along the fence.

"Good evening, Sister Cow," he said politely. "How are you keeping these days?"

"Why good evening, Brer Rabbit," said Sister Cow, looking up from the grass she was munching. "I'm keeping quite well, thank you."

"And how is Brer Bull?"

"Oh he's well enough."

Brer Rabbit paused and looked around.

"Nice place you have here," he said. "I see you have some nice apples on that tree there. They really make my mouth water after this long, hot day. I'd very much like to take one or two back home with me."

"How will you get them down?" asked Sister Cow. "They are too high for you to reach and I'm afraid I'm not too good at picking apples myself."

"I thought maybe you could butt your horns against the tree and shake some down for me," said Brer Rabbit. "Those horns of yours look in fine condition."

Now Sister Cow was very proud of her curving horns. She smiled kindly at Brer Rabbit. "Of course I will," she said. "No trouble at all."

Sister Cow walked up to the apple tree and hit it a rap with her horns—*blam!* The tree shook its leaves a little but the apples were still small and green and not one fell down. Sister Cow butted the tree again—*blim!* Still nothing fell. Next time, Sister Cow backed away across the field and took a long run at the tree, snorting crossly

as she charged. *Kerblam!* She hit the tree trunk so hard with her horns that they sank deep into the bark and stuck fast.

Sister Cow pulled and pushed and twisted and turned but it was no use. She could not move backwards or forwards or even sideways; she was quite helpless. Of course this was just what Brer Rabbit was waiting for and as soon as he was sure she was firmly stuck, he began to put his plan into effect.

"Come and help pull me out, Brer Rabbit," said Sister Cow.

"I can't climb up high enough, Sister Cow," he replied. "But hold on, don't move. I'll run and tell Brer Bull."

Brer Rabbit set off across the field for home. Before long he was back but instead of bringing Brer Bull, he had brought all his family with him—and every one of them was carrying a bucket. The bigger ones had big buckets and the little ones had little buckets and they all crowded round poor Sister Cow. The big ones milked and the little ones milked until they had milked her quite dry.

Sister Cow mooed angrily.

"I'm only thinking of you, Sister Cow," said Brer Rabbit. "You are obviously going to camp out here all night and as you won't be able to visit the milking parlor

yourself I thought I'd better help you out. I hope you're not going to be ungrateful."

Sister Cow struggled and kicked all night long but the horns were so firmly stuck into the tree that it was almost morning before at last she managed to pull herself out. Now Sister Cow was far from stupid herself. She began to work out a plan of her own.

"Brer Rabbit is sure to come by to see how I am," she thought. "And then I'll have my chance. Just wait till I get that rabbit. I'll give him apples."

Shortly before sunrise she ambled over to the apple tree and placed one horn back in the deep hole it had made. Then, with a sad, tired expression on her face, she waited.

Unfortunately for Sister Cow, Brer Rabbit was up early that morning. By the time Sister Cow had fixed her horn in the tree, Brer Rabbit was already sitting in the corner of the field and he saw the whole thing.

"Hey ho," he said to himself. "Something's going on here. Just wait there, Sister Cow, I'll be along in a moment."

He crept under the fence and out of the field. A few minutes later he came trotting down the road—*lippety-dippety*, *dippety-lippety*—whistling noisily. Sister Cow stood very still, waiting.

"Morning, Sister Cow," said Brer Rabbit, "Still there, are you?"

"I just can't get this horn loose," said Sister Cow sadly. "But if you'll come and catch hold of my tail I think we can pull it out."

Brer Rabbit came a little closer—but not too close.

"I think this is near enough, Sister Cow," he said. "I'm only a little fellow and I might get trampled. You do the pulling, Sister Cow, and I'll tell you how you're getting along."

With an angry *Moo!* Sister Cow pulled her horn out of the tree and turned to chase Brer Rabbit out of the field. Down the road they went, Brer Rabbit scampering along with his ears laid flat against his back, Sister Cow charging with her head down and her tail in the air. At last Brer Rabbit reached the briar patch. By the time Sister Cow caught up with him he was safe among the brambles, with only his head sticking out. Brer Rabbit stretched his ears up as high as he could and put on a serious face.

"Morning, Sister Cow," he said in a deep voice. "Where are you off to in such a hurry?"

"Oh, Brer Big Ears," panted Sister Cow. "Have you seen Brer Rabbit run past?"

"Why he went by just this minute," said Brer Rabbit, still in a deep voice. "And he looked mighty sick, too. If you want him you should catch up with him easily now."

With that, Sister Cow set off down the road as if ten dogs were after her while Brer Rabbit lay down there in the briar patch and rolled and laughed till his sides hurt.

Mr. Ram
makes music

One year, Mr. Benjamin Ram's wife went to stay with her mother for several months, leaving her husband all alone in their house in the middle of the forest. Mr. Ram was never lonely. Whenever anybody wanted to hold a dance or a party—which was quite often—Mr. Ram was sure to be invited, for he was the best fiddle player for miles around.

Mr. Ram was a real old-fashioned fiddle player. He could play any tune you wanted just out of his head and half the things he played he made up as he went along, tapping his foot to give a rhythm accompaniment.

One day, just before Christmastime, the whole village decided to have a party and of course they sent for Mr. Benjamin Ram to provide the music.

Mr. Ram always liked to arrive a day early for a party, to get the atmosphere right, he said. On the day before the village party the wind started howling ferociously and the sky grew black with ominous clouds. In the forest the leaves rustled and the first large raindrops fell among the undergrowth. Mr. Ram did not mind. He simply picked up his walking stick, wrapped his fiddle up in a paper bag, put on his tall hat and set out for the village. He found his way through the forest with no trouble at all, and was soon trotting along the main road towards the village. It was when he decided to take a shortcut across the fields that he began to get into difficulties. The sky grew darker and darker, the wind blew colder and colder, and at last, when he passed the same tree for the third time, Mr. Ram admitted he was lost.

Anyone else would have stopped right there and tried to work out the right road, but not Mr. Benjamin Ram. He was much too stubborn. He did not even shout to find out if anyone was near enough to hear; he simply turned round and walked on in a new direction, just as if he knew exactly where he

was going. The countryside—or what he could see through the driving rain—became more and more unfamiliar and at last Mr. Ram began to be both tired and worried.

"What if I have to spend the night all alone out here?" he thought. "And worse, what if I never get to the party and the poor folks have to do without music. Oh dear me, whatever will they do?"

Eventually he arrived at the crest of a steep hill and, looking around, he saw a light shining in the blackness, down below. With a sigh of relief he set off at a fast trot towards it. As he drew near the house where the light was, somebody shouted out: "Who's that prowling round my house?"

"It's Mr. Benjamin Ram. I'm completely lost. I just wondered if you could put me up for the night."

"Come right in, Mr. Ram. Come right in. The door's not locked."

Mr. Ram pushed the door and entered, bowing politely. Then he straightened up and glanced round the room.

"Baaaaa," cried Mr. Ram before he could stop himself. For there, right between him and the warm fire sat old Brer Wolf, flashing his brilliant white teeth in the dim light and looking decidedly hungry. If Mr. Ram had been a little younger he would have turned right round and run away as fast as his legs could carry him, but before he even had time to think, Brer Wolf had jumped over to the door, slammed it shut and padlocked it with a heavy chain.

Mr. Ram wished he was still lost in the woods but as there was little he could do, he decided to keep calm and pretend to be unworried.

"Well well, Brer Wolf, isn't it?" he said. "And how are you? Family all well are they? Good, good. I just dropped in to get myself warmed up, you know. Lost my way in the dark you see. If you'll be so kind as to point me in the direction of the village I'll be off and not disturb you anymore. They're waiting for me down there."

"Of course, Mr. Ram," said Brer Wolf, grinning widely and licking his chops. "Just

put your walking stick over there in the corner and come over to the fire for a minute. We are just ordinary working folks but anything we have is yours while you're here. We'll look after you, don't you worry." At that, Brer Wolf howled with laughter and bared his teeth so horribly that Benjamin Ram was quite unable to move.

Brer Wolf threw another log on the fire and, still laughing, went into the kitchen. Benjamin Ram, shaking with fear, could just make out the sound of Brer Wolf whispering to his wife.

"Throw away that rotten old meat—it tastes like old leather. We've some fresh meat for supper now. Delivered to the door! But be careful what you say, he's a crafty old ram."

Mrs. Wolf understood at once and said loudly: "Of course I'll cook up something for him to eat. How nice of him to drop in—and on a night like this, too. Few folks would venture out in this weather."

Then Mr. Ram heard the most sinister sound of all—the sound of a kitchen knife being sharpened on a stone, *shirrah, shirrah, shirrah.*

"Well," thought Mr. Ram stubbornly, "if I'm to go, at least I'll go to the sound of music," and he unwrapped his fiddle and began to tune the strings—*plink, plonk, plink, plonk.*

In the kitchen, Mrs. Wolf put her knife down to listen. She nudged Brer Wolf with her elbow.

"What's that noise, Brer Wolf?" she whispered.

Plink, plonk, plink, plonk went Benjamin Ram, getting the notes just right.

"I've never heard anything like it, Mrs. Wolf," said Brer Wolf. "Listen, there it goes again."

In the sitting room, Mr. Ram had tucked the fiddle under his chin, raised the bow and begun to play a merry dance tune.

"Oh, Brer Wolf, I'm scared," whispered Mrs. Wolf. "It sounds like spirit music to me."

Brer Wolf tried to look brave but he, too, was frightened. The more Mr. Ram played, the more the two wolves listened and the more frightened they became. At last Mrs. Wolf looked at Brer Wolf and Brer Wolf looked at Mrs. Wolf and without saying a word they made a bolt for the kitchen door and ran out into the woods at the back.

Mr. Ram played and played. When at last he finished, the house seemed strangely quiet. He crept to the kitchen door and peeped in. The kitchen knife lay abandoned on the table but Brer Wolf and his wife were nowhere to be seen. He looked on the back porch. No wolves. He looked in the cupboards and under the stairs. No wolves.

"Oh well," said Mr. Ram, "looks like I was wrong about Brer Wolf." Nevertheless he shut and locked all the doors and windows before he sat down to eat some bread and cheese he found in the kitchen. And he had another good look round before he fell asleep in front of the fire.

The next day Mr. Ram woke up at the crack of dawn and set off for the village. This time he found it quite easily for the main village road passed quite near to Brer Wolf's cottage.

"Where have you been, Mr. Ram?" said the villagers.

"We thought you'd got lost in the storm. But never mind, you're here—and we can have our party after all. And let's make it the best party we've ever had."

Brer Wolf breaks the law

One day after Brer Rabbit had not seen anybody for quite a long time he decided to pay a few calls. He was walking down the road on his way to visit Brer Terrapin when suddenly he heard somebody cry out:

"Help, help, please, someone help me."

Brer Rabbit stopped short and pricked up his ears.

"Who is it? What on earth is the matter?"

"Please, somebody, hurry, hurry," cried the voice.

Brer Rabbit looked all around but could see no one. "Where are you—and what are you doing there, wherever it is?" he called out.

"Please help me," said the voice. "I'm down here in the gully. And I'm stuck fast under a rock. Come and help me out before I'm crushed to death."

Brer Rabbit crept down to the edge of the big gully and looked down. There lay Brer Wolf, half-hidden under a great boulder.

In spite of having a great rock on top of him, Brer Wolf still had enough strength to shout like a sergeant but he sounded so sorry for himself that Brer Rabbit slid straight down the side of the gully to see what he could do to help.

"What can I do for you, then, Brer Wolf?" he asked. "You don't sound too happy under there."

"Please, Brer Rabbit, dear, kind Brer Rabbit, just lend a hand here and give this old rock a heave."

"Certainly, Brer Wolf," said Brer Rabbit. And he pushed at the rock until it slowly rolled off Brer Wolf's chest.

"There you are, old friend. Now, where does it hurt?"

But it turned out that Brer Wolf wasn't badly hurt at all for as soon as he was free from the boulder he grabbed Brer Rabbit by the scruff of the neck and held on tightly.

Brer Rabbit kicked and scratched, but it was no use: the more he kicked, the more

tightly Brer Wolf's teeth gripped his neck.

"That's a fine way to thank me for saving your life," panted Brer Rabbit.

Brer Wolf grinned—without loosening his teeth though.

"I'm quite happy to say thank you," he snarled. "And then I'll eat you up."

"I'll never do you another good turn as long as I live," squeaked Brer Rabbit indignantly.

"You certainly won't, Brer Rabbit. The only good turn you'll ever do anybody is to provide me with my supper."

Brer Rabbit thought quickly. "Where I come from, Brer Wolf," he said, "it's against the law for people to kill their rescuers. And I expect the law's just the same round here too."

"I don't know about that," said Brer Wolf doubtfully.

"Well I think we should make sure," said Brer Rabbit. "You don't want to go breaking any laws, now, do you? Folks can be very difficult round here. I know, let's go and ask Brer Terrapin. He's the expert. If he says it's alright to eat your rescuer for supper then you can be sure it's alright. And if he says it's all wrong, then it's all wrong and you'll get into no end of trouble."

Reluctantly Brer Wolf agreed and they set off for Brer Terrapin's house. When they found him they each presented their case. Brer Terrapin listened carefully then he put on his glasses, cleared his throat and said:

"This dispute raises many complicated legal problems. Before I can make my decision, you'll have to take me to the scene of the alleged crime."

Brer Wolf was anxious to get the matter settled so he carried Brer Terrapin on his back to the gully and pointed out the boulder. Brer Terrapin surveyed the scene from all angles, and prodded the boulder with his stick. Then he shook his head.

"I'm sorry to put you to any trouble, but there is no way out. I must see exactly how Brer Wolf was caught under the rock before I can decide."

So Brer Wolf lay down where he had been when Brer Rabbit found him and the others rolled the rock back on top of him. Brer Terrapin walked round and round and looked at Brer Wolf. Then he sat down on the rock and looked thoughtful. After a while Brer Wolf said:

"Hey, Brer Terrapin. Hurry up. This rock's beginning to crush my chest."

Brer Terrapin took no notice of him. Instead he turned to Brer Rabbit who was leaning on the rock beside him.

"Brer Rabbit, you were in the wrong," he said. "You had no business bothering Brer Wolf when he wasn't bothering you. He was just minding his own business and you should have been minding yours."

Brer Rabbit looked ashamed but Brer Terrapin had not finished.

"When you were walking down the road this morning you must have been going somewhere. If you were going somewhere then you'd better get going now." He half turned to Brer Wolf. "Brer Wolf on the other hand wasn't going anywhere. He isn't going anywhere now. You found him under that rock and that's where you should have left him. Be off now and stop pushing your nose into other people's affairs. That's my final verdict."

And with that Brer Rabbit and Brer Terrapin made off down the road, leaving Brer Wolf once again trapped under the rock.

Brer Rabbit goes fishing

Once upon a time Brer Rabbit and all the rabbits like him had long, bushy tails. Nowadays they scarcely have a tail at all. It happened like this.

One day Brer Rabbit was walking down the road shaking his fine long tail proudly from side to side. Who should he meet but Brer Fox ambling along carrying a long string of fresh fish over his shoulder.

"Morning, Brer Fox," said Brer Rabbit.

"Morning, Brer Rabbit," said Brer Fox.

"Where did you get that long string of fish, Brer Fox?"

"Caught them myself, Brer Rabbit."

"Where did you find them?"

"Down in the creek. There's plenty more, too."

"How did you set about catching them, Brer Fox? I'm mighty fond of minnows for my dinner."

Brer Fox sat down on a log by the side of the road.

"Easy, Brer Rabbit. All you have to do is wait until sundown, then go down to the edge of the water and sit on the bank with your tail hanging into the water—just as mine is hanging over this log here. During the night all the minnows will come and fix themselves onto your tail to keep themselves warm. As soon as it's daylight you can draw

65

your tail out again with as many minnows as you can carry. Any you can't manage you just throw back for another day. But you must stay there all night. If you disturb them while it's dark they'll be off before you can say 'snap'."

"Thanks for the tip, Brer Fox," said Brer Rabbit. "I'll try it out tonight."

So just after sunset Brer Rabbit crept down to the creek with a flask of hot coffee to keep him warm. He settled himself in a good place where the bulging roots of an old tree spread over the bank and sat down with his tail hanging into the water.

He sat there for hours and hours. He drank his coffee and he shivered and shook and he thought he would freeze to death.

"I had to choose the longest night of the year," he grumbled. "I'm sure last night wasn't anything like this."

But at last daylight came and Brer Rabbit was relieved to find that he was still alive.

"Fresh fish for breakfast is just what I need to warm up my old bones," he said to himself and he began to stand up stiffly to pull his tail out of the water.

"Ooooooch!" Brer Rabbit felt just as if he was splitting in two pieces for his long tail was frozen firmly into the ice. He pulled and pulled. He was trapped. He pulled again, and again. At last, with a great creak and a loud snap he was free. Brer Rabbit shot up in the air and landed again with a bump.

"Now minnows," said Brer Rabbit breathlessly, looking round for his tail. "Ouch!" screamed Brer Rabbit. For where his tail had been there was just a little cold white blob. The long bushy part was still held fast in the ice.

Actually, Brer Rabbit did not feel any pain for the whole of his back was numb with cold. But the shame of being tricked by Brer Fox was too much. Brer Rabbit limped home through the woods, making sure that no one saw him. And the strange thing is that from that day to this all the rabbits have had a little white furry stump and you won't find one anywhere with a fine bushy tail anymore.

The butter thief

One year all the animals were getting along particularly well with one another. They all drank peacefully from the same spring and they even kept their food in the same storehouse. All went well until one day someone discovered his butter had been stolen. The next day someone else complained of the same thing—and the third day it happened again. On the fourth day the animals discovered tiny footprints in the sand outside the storehouse, leading to a small hole in the wall—and leading out again.

"Our butter thief is getting careless," said Brer Fox. "I'd know those prints anywhere. They belong to young Wattle Weasel."

The animals decided that someone should stand guard all day to catch the thief and they chose Brer Mink.

"If you let him get away, no more butter for the rest of the year. Agreed?"

"Agreed," said all the animals.

Next day Brer Mink stayed on guard while the rest of the animals went about their business. Brer Mink watched and listened and he watched and waited. He sat so still that eventually he felt cramps in his legs but he dared not move. Just then little Wattle Weasel popped his head under the door.

"Hey, Brer Mink," he squeaked. "You look pretty lonely in there. Why don't you come out and play a game of hide and seek?"

"He can hardly steal the butter if he's playing with me," said Brer Mink to himself, and without another thought he ran out into the sunshine.

Brer Mink and Wattle Weasel played hide and seek all round the storehouse until finally Brer Mink was so tired he could not run anymore.

"I really must rest a minute, Wattle," he panted.

"Me too," said Wattle Weasel.

Both animals lay down by the storehouse

door and Brer Mink immediately fell fast asleep. But little Wattle Weasel crept through the hole in the wall and helped himself to as much butter as he could manage.

Of course when the other animals came back and saw what had happened, Brer Mink was sent home in disgrace. Next day Brer Possum was left to guard the butter. Brer Possum sat and watched and he sat and waited. After a while little Wattle Weasel came by.

"How are you, Brer Possum?" he said, slapping him lightly on the back. Now Brer Possum was very ticklish and as soon as Wattle Weasel's paws touched his fur he began to giggle. Wattle Weasel kept on tickling him until Brer Possum was quite breathless. Then Wattle Weasel left him lying collapsed on the ground and helped himself to as much butter as he could manage.

Next day Brer Raccoon was on guard. He had hardly settled himself comfortably when Wattle Weasel appeared.

"Race you to the river, Brer Raccoon," said Wattle.

Brer Raccoon could not resist a challenge so off they went. Brer Raccoon followed the path but cunning Wattle Weasel knew all the shortcuts and before Brer Raccoon realized he had been tricked, Wattle Weasel had doubled back to the storehouse and helped himself to as much butter as he could manage.

Next day Brer Bear was on guard. Brer Bear was pleased. Sitting in the sun was much better than digging and he settled down feeling very contented. Soon Wattle Weasel arrived.

"Hello, Brer Bear. How are you these days?" he said.

"Hello, Wattle," said Brer Bear, watching very carefully.

"Oh, what was that, Brer Bear?"said Wattle. "I thought I saw a flea jump onto your back. Just let me have a look for you."

Then Wattle climbed onto Brer Bear's back and began to rub his neck and scratch his sides. It wasn't long before Brer Bear was stretched out fast asleep, snoring like a sawmill. Little Wattle Weasel helped himself to as much butter as he could manage.

At last the animals sent for Brer Rabbit.

"He's our last hope," said Brer Buzzard. "That is if he doesn't eat it all himself."

Next day Brer Rabbit arrived early at the storehouse. He had a good look round then took a piece of string out of his pocket and hid himself behind a sack of carrots, making sure he had a good view of the butter.

It was not long before Wattle Weasel arrived, looked round, sniffed and made straight for his favorite food.

"Leave that butter alone," shouted Brer Rabbit. Wattle jumped back as if he had been burned.

"That must be Brer Rabbit," he said. And

he began to figure ways to trick him.

"Just leave that butter alone," said Brer Rabbit sternly.

"Can't I even have a little bit to taste?" asked Wattle.

"No," said Brer Rabbit.

"Well now that I'm here, we might as well have a game," said Wattle. "What about a race?"

"I'm too tired," said Brer Rabbit crossly.

"Well hide and seek then."

"I'm too old for kids' games."

"I could give your back a good rub."

"My back's quite all right, thank you. But I tell you what," said Brer Rabbit, "I'll take your tail and tie it up and you can take mine and tie it up—then we'll pull against each other and see who is the strongest."

Now Wattle Weasel knew what a small, weak tail Brer Rabbit had but he didn't know how good Brer Rabbit was at tricking people. So he agreed to the game and they tied up each other's tails with Brer Rabbit's piece of string.

"You stand inside," said Brer Rabbit, "and I'll stand outside and we'll pull and pull as hard as we can."

"Done," said Wattle cheerfully.

As soon as Brer Rabbit was outside, he slipped easily out of the string and tied it round a tree root instead. Then he crept back and peeped round the door. Wattle tugged and pulled and puffed and panted. Finally he said:

"Come and untie me, Brer Rabbit. You win. I can't pull anymore."

Brer Rabbit poked his whiskers round the door. "I never said I'd untie you, Wattle," he laughed. "That's for the others to decide."

When the other animals came to see what had happened, there was Wattle Weasel, still tied fast by the tail, looking very sorry for himself.

"I'll never steal anything ever again," he whined. "And butter—ugh—I'll never taste another bite."

As for Brer Rabbit, he was the hero of the village—at least for a day or two.

Brer Fox goes hunting

While Brer Rabbit was the hero of the whole village Brer Fox, not wanting to miss out on anything, decided to make friends with him. At first both animals acted in a very cautious way but after a time they began to relax and before very long they were calling on each other as if there had never been any trouble between them.

One day Brer Fox came to Brer Rabbit's house with a very purposeful look on his face. Brer Rabbit was lounging in a chair on the porch, his eyes half-closed.

"You look busy, Brer Fox," said Brer Rabbit, settling himself back more comfortably.

"I'm going hunting, Brer Rabbit," said Brer Fox. "Care to come along?"

"Not today, thanks," said Brer Rabbit, who was feeling rather lazy. "I'm busy planning my work program for the next month. I can't put it off any longer."

"That's a pity," said Brer Fox, "because it looks like a good day for hunting. Never mind, I'll go myself anyway. Anything I can bring you back, Brer Rabbit?"

"Not a thing, Brer Fox," replied Brer Rabbit. "Thanks all the same. Have a good day."

Brer Fox spent all day in the woods and by the time evening came he had caught a great bagful of game.

"This should keep us going for a few days," he said happily to himself as he set out for home.

At just about the same time, Brer Rabbit awoke from his afternoon doze, stretched his legs, rubbed his eyes and smoothed his whiskers.

"Brer Fox should be on the way home by now," he said to himself, and he clambered onto a tree stump to see what he could see. He had not been there very long when, sure enough, along came Brer Fox, singing to himself and swinging the bag of game from his shoulder. Quickly Brer

Rabbit jumped off the tree stump, ran down the road a little way and lay down in the middle of the track pretending to be dead.

"What's this rabbit doing here?" asked Brer Fox as he came up. He turned Brer Rabbit over with his foot. "This rabbit's dead. And he looks as if he's been dead for some time, too." He prodded Brer Rabbit with his stick. "He may be dead, but he's the fattest rabbit I've ever seen. But he's been dead too long. It's not safe to take him home."

Brer Rabbit held his breath and said nothing. Brer Fox licked his lips and lingered a few moments longer but at last he went off, leaving the rabbit lying in the road.

As soon as Brer Fox was out of sight, Brer Rabbit jumped up and ran through the woods so that he was in front of Brer Fox once more. He lay down in the road, as still as still could be. Soon Brer Fox came walking along. There lay Brer Rabbit, in his path, apparently cold and stiff.

Brer Fox stopped and stared. He scratched his head. He stood gazing at Brer Rabbit for a long time, thinking hard. Then he looked suspiciously all around. After a while he took the bag of game off

his shoulder and said to himself: "These rabbits are going to waste. It's a crime to leave them lying here to rot." He looked round again and poked Brer Rabbit's fat body with his foot. "Another fat one, too, by the look of it. No, it's too good to miss. I'll just leave my bag here and run back to fetch that other rabbit. After all, there's no sense turning down a free gift, is there?"

With that he abandoned the sack of game and loped back up the road towards the place where he had seen the first rabbit.

As soon as Brer Fox was out of sight, Brer Rabbit jumped up, snatched the bag of game and made off for home at top speed.

Next time Brer Rabbit saw Brer Fox, Brer Fox was not looking very friendly at all.

"What did you catch the other day?" asked Brer Rabbit innocently.

Brer Fox scratched his head thoughtfully.

"I caught a handful of hard sense, Brer Rabbit," he said, scowling.

Brer Rabbit laughed. "If I'd known that was what you were after, Brer Fox, I'd have loaned you some of mine," he chuckled.

After that, Brer Fox forgot about being friendly with Brer Rabbit. As for Brer Rabbit, he went on making mischief as he had always done.

Brer Rabbit and the jar of honey

One day Brer Rabbit decided to visit Brer Bear's house to see what he could find. He waited outside until he saw the whole bear family walk down the path—old Brer Bear with Mrs. Bear in front, and their twin sons Kubs and Klibs shuffling and scrambling along behind. As soon as they were out of the gate, Brer Rabbit hopped up to the house, opened the door and began searching around, just like a burglar.

He was looking at this and sticking his nose into that when he knocked over an enormous pot of honey that Brer Bear had hidden on a high shelf in a cupboard. Down flowed the honey, all over Brer Rabbit, nearly drowning him in thick, sticky liquid. In a moment, poor Brer Rabbit was covered in honey from head to toes—all over. He had to sit and wait for it to drip off his head before he could even see what was going on and when he tried to wipe it off, his hands just became tangled in sticky fur.

"Help," said Brer Rabbit through a mouthful of honey. "What am I going to do now? If I go outside, the bees will swarm all over me and sting me to death. And if I stay here, Brer Bear will come back and beat me up. Whatever can I do?"

However, Brer Rabbit was not someone who gave up easily and after a while he had an idea. He hopped to the door and then made a quick dash to the woods behind the house. There he rolled over and over in the dead, dry leaves, trying to scrub and rub the honey off. The plan did not work quite as he had intended. Instead of getting rid of the honey, he became covered in leaves! The more he rolled the more the leaves stuck to him until he looked like the most horrible animal you have ever seen, thickly covered with dark, scaly leaves and still oozing honey from his fur. Brer Rabbit jumped up and down desperately trying to shake off the leaves but it was no use. The leaves stuck fast. He shook and shivered. The leaves

stuck fast. He capered and stamped and danced with rage. Still the leaves stuck fast. Finally he decided the only thing he could do was to make his way home as fast as he could and get some help from his family.

The first person Brer Rabbit met was Sister Cow and as soon as she set eyes on him she fled as if a pack of dogs was after her. Brer Rabbit began to laugh. If a sedate old lady like Sister Cow kicked up her heels and ran off like that in broad daylight then he must look a very strange sight indeed.

"Maybe I'll get some fun out of this after all," he thought, feeling quite pleased with himself again. "Maybe I'll drop round on Brer Fox and see what he thinks of my new outfit."

While he was thinking about this, up came Brer Bear, still with Mrs. Bear and the two cubs. Brer Rabbit sidled towards them. Brer Bear stopped to have a good look. Brer Rabbit edged closer and closer, the sticky leaves making a sinister *swishy-swushy, splushy-splishy* sound as he moved.

Mrs. Bear stood it as long as she could but as the apparition came nearer she dropped her parasol in the road, and ran to climb the nearest tree. Brer Bear looked as though he was going to stand his ground but Brer Rabbit suddenly leaped high in the air and gave an unearthly scream. That was too much for Brer Bear and he also made a run for it, crashing into the fence and knocking down a whole section as he went. As for the two children, Kubs and Klibs, they stamped through the bushes like a herd of baby elephants.

Now thoroughly pleased with life, Brer Rabbit paraded on proudly along the road. After a while he came upon Brer Fox and Brer Wolf. They were plotting together to think up a way to catch Brer Rabbit and were so involved in their schemes that they did not notice him until he was just about on top of them.

Brer Fox immediately put his tail between his legs and turned to run off. Brer Wolf, wanting to look brave in front of Brer Fox, stood his ground.

"Who are you?" he demanded with a growl.

Brer Rabbit leaped up and down in the road, waving his arms and shrieking: "I'm the devil, I'm the devil. I've come to take you away."

This time, even Brer Wolf turned and fled.

It took Brer Rabbit several days to clean all the honey and leaves from his fur and he kept well out of sight until he looked normal again, but for a long time afterwards he used to hide behind a tree if he saw Brer Fox and Brer Wolf coming. As they passed by he would jump out shouting: "I'm the devil, I'm the devil," and roar with laughter as he watched them scamper away as fast as their legs would carry them.

Brer Fox catches a thief

One year Brer Fox decided to plant a peanut patch in his garden. He broke up the ground and planted several rows of peanuts. Brer Rabbit used to hop past every day to watch Brer Fox at work and when he got home he would wink one eye knowingly and say to his children:

"You plant it in the ground
It grows so free
Who'll pick it out?
Just wait and see."

Sure enough, when the peanuts began to ripen, every time Brer Fox went to pick some of them he found someone had been there before him, grubbing away among the vines and picking out all the ripe nuts. Brer Fox was very very cross. He suspected who the someone was but old Brer Rabbit covered his tracks so well that Brer Fox didn't know how he could catch him.

One day Brer Fox was taking a walk all round the peanut patch and it wasn't long before he found a crack in the fence where the rail had been rubbed really smooth. That's where he decided to set his trap. A strong young tree was growing in the corner by the hole in the fence. Brer Fox jumped up and caught the tip of one of its branches and bent it right down to the ground. Holding the branch steady with his long teeth, he tied one end of a strong rope to it. He made the other end of the rope into a kind of noose and then wedged the branch tip firmly into the crack in the fence.

Next morning Brer Rabbit came skipping along just as Brer Fox had expected. He crept through the crack. When he was half-way through his foot touched the wedge holding the branch down. All at once the sapling sprang up, the noose tightened around his body and there was Brer Rabbit, hanging half-way between Heaven and Earth. There he swung, afraid that he might fall any moment—and just as afraid that he might not fall at all.

While he was deciding what story he would tell Brer Fox he heard someone lumbering along the road and presently old Brer Bear came ambling along. Brer Bear was in a good mood because he had just found a new honey tree.

"Howdy, Brer Bear," said Brer Rabbit. Brer Bear looked all around.

"Up here," said Brer Rabbit as casually as he could.

"What are you doing up there?" asked Brer Bear.

"I'm doing all right, Brer Bear," said Brer Rabbit. "I'm earning myself a dollar a minute up here."

"How are you doing that, Brer Rabbit?"

"I'm keeping the crows off Brer Fox's peanut patch. Why don't you have a try, Brer Bear? It's easy money and I know you've a big family to take care of. Share and share alike, that's what I say. Besides, you'd make such a nice scarecrow."

"That's very kind, Brer Rabbit. And you're right, I could use a few dollars."

So Brer Rabbit explained how Brer Bear should bend down the branch and before long Brer Bear was up there swinging in Brer Rabbit's place. Brer Rabbit went straight over to Brer Fox's house.

"Brer Fox, oh Brer Fox," he shouted. "Come out here, Brer Fox, and I'll show you who's been stealing your peanuts."

Brer Fox grabbed his walking stick and they both ran back to the peanut patch. When they arrived, sure enough, there was Brer Bear hanging from the branch, peering round for crows.

"So I've caught you, have I?" cried Brer Fox and before Brer Bear had a chance to explain, Brer Rabbit began to jump up and down shouting: "Hit him, Brer Fox, hit him."

Brer Fox raised a stick and—*blip*—he brought it down on Brer Bear's back and every time Brer Bear opened his mouth to explain, Brer Fox hit him again.

While all this was going on, Brer Rabbit slipped away and hid in a deep pool of mud by the road with only his eyes sticking out.

He knew Brer Bear would come after him. Sure enough, by and by Brer Bear came limping down the road and when he reached the mud pool he stopped.

"Howdy, Brer Frog," he said. "Have you seen Brer Rabbit go past here?"

"He just went by," said Brer Rabbit and old Brer Bear lumbered off down the road like a frightened mule.

As soon as he was out of sight Brer Rabbit hopped out of the mud, washed himself in the nearby stream and lay out in the sun to dry himself. But he never went back to Brer Fox's peanut patch!

The moon in the millpond

One day after there had been no trouble between any of the animals for some time Brer Rabbit began to feel rather mischievous. He did not like peace and quiet. It made him sit around and put on weight. And, he claimed, sooner or later the lack of activity would affect his ability to think quickly.

On this particular day, after supper, Brer Rabbit met Brer Terrapin and they sat down by the side of the road to chat about the good old days.

"To tell you the truth, Brer Terrapin, I am sick and tired of everyone getting on so well. What we need is a bit of fun to wake us all up."

Brer Terrapin agreed.

"I know," said Brer Rabbit, "let's tell Brer Fox, Brer Wolf and Brer Bear to meet us tomorrow night down at the millpond. We can all go fishing. I'll arrange it all. You just turn up."

Brer Rabbit scampered off home feeling better already and Brer Terrapin set off slowly for the millpond. "After all, if I'm going to be there for tomorrow evening," he thought, "I'd better start in good time."

The next day Brer Rabbit sent messages to Brer Fox, Brer Bear and Brer Wolf who all thought fishing in the millpond a very good idea—simply because it had never occurred to any of them before. They all arrived in time. Brer Bear and Brer Wolf brought hooks and lines, Brer Fox brought a net and Brer Terrapin, not to be outdone, had managed to find some bait.

"I'm trying for a good fat pike," said Brer Bear.

"I prefer trout," said Brer Wolf.

"I'm after perch," said Brer Fox.

"I think I'll catch minnows," said Brer Terrapin.

"I'm going for suckers," whispered Brer Rabbit, giving Brer Terrapin a broad wink.

When they were all ready, Brer Rabbit went to the edge of the pond to cast the first line. Suddenly he jumped back in surprise. He dropped his rod and stood there looking into the water, scratching his head.

"What is it?" asked the others.

Brer Rabbit just stood there looking confused. Finally he took a deep breath and said: 'Gentlemen, we might as well give up fishing here. There's nothing in that pond for any of us tonight."

Brer Terrapin joined Brer Rabbit at the edge of the pond and he, too, looked into the water.

"Brer Rabbit's quite right," he said wisely. "You'd better all go home before anything dangerous happens."

"Don't be frightened," said Brer Rabbit. "Accidents will happen and, well, there's nothing much wrong except, er, the moon has fallen into the pond. If you don't believe me, look for yourself."

Brer Fox, Brer Bear and Brer Wolf approached the edge of the pond cautiously. Sure enough there, at the bottom of the pond, lay the moon, shimmering slightly through the ripples in the water. Everybody had a good look.

"Well, well, well," said Brer Fox.

"Mighty bad, mighty bad,"said Brer Wolf.

"Oh dear," said Brer Bear.

Brer Rabbit thought for a moment. "Gentlemen, what we need here is action. Unless we get that moon out of the pond we'll have spent a completely wasted evening because you'll never find any fish where there's a moon swimming about."

"What can we do about it?" asked Brer Fox.

"Better ask Brer Rabbit," said Brer Terrapin. "He usually has a plan for everything."

Brer Rabbit shut his eyes and looked wise. "It seems to me," he said at last, "that the easiest way out of this difficulty is to get a good strong fishing net from somewhere. Yours isn't nearly strong enough, Brer Fox. That moon looks delicate but it must weigh hundreds of pounds. I'll just run round to Mr. Mud Turtle's place and borrow his net." And he ran off into the darkness.

"Seems to me," said Brer Terrapin half to himself, "that there's some money to be made out of this moon."

"What's that?" asked Brer Fox sharply.

"Seems to me," repeated Brer Terrapin, "that anyone who owns a real solid moon like that could sell it for a whole heap of money. Enough to live on comfortably for the rest of his life, I shouldn't wonder."

Brer Fox looked at Brer Wolf and Brer Wolf looked at Brer Bear.

"Doesn't look too difficult, either," went on Brer Terrapin.

Just then Brer Rabbit reappeared carrying a large, heavy net. He began to take off his coat and to roll up his trousers.

"No, no, Brer Rabbit," cried Brer Fox. "We can't let you get your feet wet, I know how much you hate water. Here, let us do it."

So Brer Fox and Brer Wolf each took one end of the net and waded out into the water. Brer Bear splashed in after them holding the edge to make sure it did not get caught in the rushes. They threw the net into the middle of the pond and pulled it eagerly in. No moon. They threw it out again. Still no moon. Each time they waded out farther and farther from the edge of the pond until the water came up first to their waists, then all the way up to their necks. Before very long they reached the point where the bottom of the pond started to shelve deeply. Brer Fox stepped right off the shelf and suddenly disappeared. A few seconds later Brer Wolf also vanished, closely followed—with an enormous splash—by Brer Bear.

All three came up again spluttering and floundering, making such great waves that it looked as if all the water would splash right out of the pond. The moon, broken into a thousand glimmering pieces, flickered over the surface.

When the three finally emerged from the water Brer Rabbit and Brer Terrapin were nowhere to be seen, but as the dripping, bedraggled animals made for home they heard a mocking voice calling: "I hear the best way to hook the moon is to use fools for bait."

Brer Fox loses his supper

One day Brer Fox and Brer Rabbit stole a large joint of meat from Mr. Man's house. They carried it into the woods nearby and started to discuss the next move.

"I think we'd better try it," said Brer Fox.

"Why not?" said Brer Rabbit.

So Brer Fox gnawed off a great hunk, shut both eyes contentedly and began to chew. He chewed and tasted and tasted and chewed. Brer Rabbit just sat there and watched. Eventually Brer Fox smacked his lips and said: "Brer Rabbit, this is lamb."

"Surely not, Brer Fox."

"It's lamb, I tell you, Brer Rabbit."

"Never," said Brer Rabbit.

Then Brer Rabbit gnawed a piece of meat and chewed it.

"Brer Fox, this is pork," said Brer Rabbit.

"Brer Rabbit, you're fooling me," said Brer Fox.

"I swear it's pork, Brer Fox."

"It couldn't be."

"It is, I tell you."

So they chewed and argued and argued and chewed. After some time Brer Rabbit pretended he wanted a drink of water and he rushed off into the bushes. He came back wiping his mouth.

"Where did you find water?" asked Brer Fox, feeling thirsty himself.

"Across the road, down that hill and up the little gully," said Brer Rabbit.

Off went Brer Fox, across the road and down the hill but he could not see any sign of a gully or a spring. Eventually he came to a small valley but there was no sign of any water there.

While Brer Fox was running round looking for the spring, Brer Rabbit quickly dug a hole in the ground and hid the meat, covering it over with twigs and grasses. Next he cut himself a long whip out of a piece of wood. Soon he heard Brer Fox coming back. Brer Rabbit hid in a clump of bushes nearby and began to hit a small tree with the whip he had made. Every time he hit the tree, he cried out as if his life was in danger.

Pow! pow! went the stick.

"Oh, please, Mr. Man."

Pow! Pow!

"Oh please Mr. Man."

Pow!

"Oh I beg you Mr. Man. I didn't take your meat."

Pow!

"Please Mr. Man, it wasn't me. It was Brer Fox who stole your meat."

Brer Fox stopped to listen. Every time he heard the whip hit the tree he grinned and said to himself: "Serves you right you troublemaking rabbit. You tricked me with the water—you deserve everything you get."

After quite some time the noise died down and it sounded as though Mr. Man was dragging Brer Rabbit off. Then nothing. Brer Fox began to feel a little nervous. He looked around cautiously. Suddenly, Brer Rabbit burst from the bushes looking terrified and screaming: "Run, Brer Fox, run. Mr. Man is coming to get you. Run for your life. He's got a gun, Brer Fox."

And Brer Fox ran—leaving all the meat to a very satisfied Brer Rabbit.

Brer Rabbit builds a tower

One day the animals decided that Brer Rabbit had really made too much trouble for everyone and they called a meeting to decide what to do.

"There's only one thing we can do," said Brer Wolf. "Keep him right away from us."

"Don't let him drink from our stream," said Mr. Wildcat.

"Don't let him walk on our road," said Brer Bear.

"Don't let him live in our village," said Brer Fox.

"Don't let him use our washing hole," said Sister Cow.

Brer Rabbit was not really worried by the decision but just in case there was any trouble he started to strengthen his house. He repaired all the locks and bolts on the doors, put up shutters at the windows and mended the fence around the garden. Then he started to build a tower on top of the house. The tower rose higher and higher until the villagers began to stop on the road and ask what the strange new building was.

Brer Rabbit had no time to explain. He hammered and sawed and knocked and nailed. The villagers passed by; Brer Rabbit did not even look up. They stood to watch him work; he just went on hammering. It was work, work, work from sunrise to sunset until the tower was finished.

Then Brer Rabbit took a deep breath, wiped his forehead and said to himself: "Right. Now let them come and get me if they can."

Then he fetched a long piece of strong rope, called for a meal and went to sit in his rocking chair looking out of the tower window.

"Now listen carefully," he said to his wife. "Put the kettle of water on the fire to boil and stand close by me here. Anything I ask you to do, do it right away. Then we'll see some fun."

It was not long before all the animals heard that Brer Rabbit had finished working and they began to gather round to see what he would do next. Brer Wolf stood looking up at the tower with Brer Fox beside him. The others stood about looking up, too. They walked round and round, they changed places to get a better view and they looked and they looked and they looked.

Brer Rabbit sat in the window chewing a lettuce leaf, taking no notice of the crowd below him.

After a while Brer Terrapin came along. Now Brer Terrapin knew exactly how Brer Rabbit's mind worked and he realized that something interesting was going to happen before the end of the day.

"Heyo, Brer Rabbit! What are you doing up in the clouds like that?" he shouted.

"I'm staying up here for my health, Brer Terrapin," said Brer Rabbit. "Why don't you drop up to see me?"

"Between you and me, Brer Rabbit, dropping down looks easier than dropping up. Why don't you come down to see me? Anyone who lives as high up as that needs wings and I'm no high flier myself. I'm frightened to shake hands with you all the way up there."

"Don't worry, Brer Terrapin. I've a kind of moving staircase here and I'll just let it down to you." Brer Rabbit let down the rope. "Just catch hold of that and up you come as easy as a bird."

Brer Terrapin knew Brer Rabbit had nothing against him but he was a cautious creature so he caught hold of the rope in his mouth and tested the strength of it.

"Seems all right," he muttered, and holding on firmly with his mouth and feet he called: "Pull away, Brer Rabbit, pull away."

"Hold tight," replied Brer Rabbit and the animals watched as Brer Terrapin swung round and round, higher and higher to the window in the tower. Before long he was sitting there beside Brer Rabbit, eating and drinking contentedly.

When the other animals saw Brer Terrapin enjoying himself they wanted to see the inside of Brer Rabbit's tower for themselves.

Brer Wolf was the first to speak.

"Hey there, Brer Rabbit. You look mighty comfortable up there. How are you today?"

Brer Rabbit looked down to see who was calling. "I'm not so well, Brer Wolf," he shouted, "but at least I still have my appetite." He took another bite of lettuce. "Won't you come up and see me?"

"It looks like a hard journey," said Brer Wolf, "but I'm no coward: I'll take a little risk to see you."

So Brer Rabbit let down the rope again and Brer Wolf caught hold of it. Slowly, he began to swing upwards towards the tower. He had almost reached the window when he heard Brer Rabbit shouting: "Hurry up, wife, and set the table. We've a visitor on the way. But before you do that, bring the kettle to make the coffee."

Still Brer Wolf swung slowly upwards.

"Look out!" cried Brer Rabbit. "Be careful or you'll spill that boiling water on Brer Wolf!"

Those were the last words Brer Wolf heard for the next minute a stream of boiling water hit him right on the back of the neck. He gave a howl of pain, let go of the rope and fell straight down to the ground, bouncing like a rubber ball as he hit the grass.

"My, Brer Wolf," shouted Brer Rabbit, "how careless of my wife. I must apologize for her, she's so clumsy. Are you all right down there, Brer Wolf? Nothing broken, I hope. And I do hope the hair will grow again on that sore spot on your neck. A wolf with a bald patch will certainly look a bit odd."

Brer Wolf scowled angrily and limped away to his house. High above him, Brer Rabbit and Brer Terrapin, shaking with laughter, settled down to finish their meal.

Brer Rabbit and the little girl

One day when Brer Rabbit was hunting around for some salad to eat for his supper, he found himself outside Mr. Man's house. He hopped cautiously along outside the garden fence until he came to the gate. Inside was a little girl playing in the sand, and behind her was a whole garden full of the most delicious looking cabbages and lettuces. Brer Rabbit's mouth began to water at the sight and he stood peering through the bars of the gate. Then, being as polite and humble as he knew how, he said:

"Hello, little girl. And how are you today?"

"Hello," said the little girl. "I'm very well thank you. How are you?"

"Unfortunately I'm not so well myself at all," said Brer Rabbit weakly. "But never mind that. Are you the daughter of the man who lives in that big white house there?"

"Yes I am," said the little girl.

"Well what a lucky coincidence," said Brer Rabbit. "I've just met your father down the road and he said I should tell you to open the gate for me and give me some of those greens growing there."

The little girl opened the gate at once and Brer Rabbit hopped in. Brer Rabbit did not waste any time. He hopped right over to the vegetable patch, picked as many vegetables as he could carry and hopped back down the path.

"Thank you very much, little girl," he said politely—and ran for home.

Next day Brer Rabbit hid near the fence until he saw the little girl come out to play again. Brer Rabbit told her the same story, once again she opened the gate and he went happily home with a feast of green vegetables. He came the next day, too, and the one after that and each time he took home as much as he could carry.

Before long, Mr. Man began to notice how bare his garden was looking. As the days passed, he grew more and more worried and he started to accuse everyone of stealing his vegetables.

"But Pa," said the little girl, "Mr. Rabbit told me you said he could have the lettuces and things. So I let him into the garden and he's the one that took the vegetables."

Mr. Man guessed what had happened. He laughed.

"Gracious me, I'd quite forgotten about Mr. Rabbit. Of course, that's the answer. Now remember, the next time Mr. Rabbit comes, let him in as usual but run as fast as you can and tell me he's here because I have some business to attend to with that fellow."

Sure enough, next morning the little girl was playing in the garden when Brer Rabbit came to collect his daily ration. The little girl opened the gate as soon as she saw him, then ran up to the house.

"Pa, Pa. Brer Rabbit's in the garden now if you want him," she cried.

Mr. Man stopped what he was doing, grabbed a fishing line from the cupboard and rushed down to the garden. Brer Rabbit was too busy frolicking among the strawberries and squashing the tomato plants to notice what was going on until Mr. Man was almost on top of him. Then he tried to hide behind a large cabbage leaf—but it was too late. In a flash, Mr. Man had grabbed Brer Rabbit by the ears and before you could say 'greens', Brer Rabbit was

bound hand and foot with the fishing line. After he had tightened all the knots to make quite sure Brer Rabbit could not escape, Mr. Man stood up.

"You've fooled me time and time again, Brer Rabbit, but now its my turn to pay *you* back. I'm going to teach you a lesson you'll never forget and when I've finished we're going to eat you for supper."

With that Mr. Man called his daughter to guard Brer Rabbit and stamped off angrily up the garden path.

Brer Rabbit stayed very quiet until Mr. Man was out of earshot. Then, to the little girl's surprise he began to sing. In those days Brer Rabbit was a very good singer, though not many people were aware of the fact. The little girl was delighted and as soon as he had finished she begged him to sing some more.

Brer Rabbit coughed harshly. "Oh I don't think I can sing any more, little girl. You know I haven't been at all well and I don't want to damage my chest."

"Oh please, Brer Rabbit. Just one more."

"Impossible, I'm afraid. I could dance for you instead of course. There's nothing wrong with my legs and you may not believe it but I dance even better than I sing."

"Yes please, Brer Rabbit. Oh yes, do dance. I'd like that."

"Not possible, unfortunately."

"Oh please," said the little girl.

"Just look at me. How do you think I can dance trussed up like this? I can hardly waggle my ears let alone move my legs."

"Let me untie you, then," said the little girl.

"You can if you like," said Brer Rabbit coolly.

The little girl bent down and untied all the knots in the fishing line—and Brer Rabbit was free again. He looked round cautiously for any sign of Mr. Man, but he was still busy in the house. Brer Rabbit did a rapid pirouette.

"Just watch me dance, little girl," he shouted as he raced for the garden gate.

And Brer Rabbit danced all the way home.

Brer Rabbit goes shopping

One year Brer Rabbit grew a fine crop of peanuts. He promised himself that if he managed to sell them for as much money as he thought they were worth, then he would be able to go out and buy all the little household things that his family had had to do without for so long.

As soon as he told Mrs. Rabbit what he was going to do, she had some ideas of her own.

"You must buy seven tin cups for the children to drink out of and seven tin plates for the children's food—and there's the coffeepot we've been needing so badly."

"That's exactly what I'm intending to buy," said Brer Rabbit.

As soon as Brer Rabbit had left the house Mrs. Rabbit popped across the road to see her neighbor Mrs. Mink. Mrs. Rabbit began to boast about what Brer Rabbit was going to do. So when poor old Brer Mink came home, Mrs. Mink nagged away at him to go and earn some money to make life a little easier for her.

"If Brer Rabbit can do it for his wife, I'm sure you can manage something for me," she said. They quarrelled all night after that. Next day Mrs. Mink went round to see Mrs. Fox and passed on the news to her. When Brer Fox came home that night, he was in trouble too.

"You're nothing but a lazy good-for-nothing," said his wife. "Fancy Brer Rabbit getting all those fancy plates and cups while we eat off any old thing."

After that the news spread like wildfire through the neighborhood. Mrs. Fox told Mrs. Wolf, who told Mrs. Bear—and soon everyone knew about Brer Rabbit's new-found wealth. Husbands and wives hardly spoke to one another anymore and even the children began to complain that Brer Rabbit's children were better treated than they were.

Brer Fox, Brer Wolf and Brer Bear had

spent the whole year trying to outwit Brer Rabbit and they decided that this was a perfect opportunity to get even— especially as Brer Rabbit was making their homelives so miserable. They agreed to hide beside the road from town and catch Brer Rabbit as he returned loaded with his cups and plates and his new coffeepot.

Next Wednesday, soon after breakfast, Brer Rabbit set off for town. He sold his crop for even more money than he expected and managed to buy a new pair of braces for himself as well as the coffeepot, the plates and cups and a scarf for his wife.

He finished his shopping just after lunch and, feeling very pleased with himself, he set off for home. After he had been walking for quite a long time he began to feel a bit tired, so he sat down. He was just settling down with his back to a tree to rest when he saw three strange marks in the sand beside him.

"Hmm," said Brer Rabbit. "That looks like the mark of Brer Fox's nice bushy tail to me. And this one must be Brer Wolf's

fine long tail. And this one, why that's where Brer Bear squatted down on his haunches for there's no sign of a tail at all. Where those three animals sit together there's bound to be trouble. And if I'm not mistaken it's trouble for me this time. If I'm right they'll be waiting for me down there in the hollow."

Very quietly Brer Rabbit clambered up the bank beside the road and hopped up to the top of a small hill to get a better view. Sure enough there, in the hollow, were three familiar shapes. Brer Fox was crouched on one side of the road, Brer Wolf on the other while Brer Bear was curled up in the ditch taking a nap in the sun. Brer Rabbit nearly laughed out loud but just managed to cover his mouth with his hand in time. He crept back to where he had left his parcels and began to dress himself up in a very curious fashion. He turned the coffee-pot upside down and put it on his head; he ran a piece of string through the handles of the cups and slung the whole lot over his shoulder. Finally he picked up the plates and, carrying some in one hand and some in the other, crept up to the top of the small hill again.

Everything was quiet and still in the midday heat. Even the grasshoppers were silent. So when Brer Rabbit let out a great whoop and set off down the hillside waving his arms he made a really terrible noise— *Rickety, rackety slambang!* went the plates. *Rickety, rackety slambang!* went the cups.

Brer Fox and Brer Wolf, waiting patiently in the midday sun, sprang to their feet and began to growl fiercely at the amazing sound and sight of Brer Rabbit. Old Brer Bear woke with a start and was so terrified by the banging that he rushed wildly out of the ditch and fell right over Brer Fox in his hurry. And when he saw what he thought was some strange monster coming straight for him at top speed, he whirled right round in the road again and blundered straight into Brer Wolf! By the time they had all sorted themselves out there was Brer Rabbit almost on top of them.

85

"Make way, make way," shouted Brer Rabbit, rattling his cups and plates. "I'm tin-tinker the iron man. Watch out for my iron claws. Watch out for my iron teeth."

Rickety, rackety slambang! went the cups. *Rickety, rackety slambang!* went the plates. In a flurry of noise and confusion, Brer Rabbit disappeared round a bend in the road.

"Let's get out of here," cried Brer Fox and Brer Wolf, speeding off in opposite directions as fast as their legs could carry them. Brer Bear was not so lucky. Still half–dazed with sleep he blundered off the road straight into a pile of brushwood that had been left beside an old tree stump.

Since none of the other animals dared to return to that spot for some time, Brer Rabbit and his family had a good supply of firewood all to themselves.

Brer Bear tests his strength

One day the animals were sitting talking under the big tree. Brer Rabbit was lounging against a big root. Brer Fox sat next to Brer Wolf in a deep patch of shade and Brer Bear was leaning with his broad back against the trunk of the tree. In the middle was Brer Terrapin, perched on a rocking chair. After a time the animals began to boast about what they could do.

"Whatever you may have seen," said Brer Rabbit, "I'm the swiftest one here."

Brer Terrapin smiled and rocked in the chair.

"I'm the sharpest," said Brer Fox. "Nothing much escapes my notice. If I miss something, you can take it from me it's not worth catching."

Brer Terrapin smiled and went on rocking.

"I'm the most savage," growled Brer Wolf. "Even people are afraid of me."

Brer Terrapin rocked a little more.

"I may not look fierce," said Brer Bear, "but if you put me to the test you'll find I'm the strongest of you all."

Brer Terrapin went on rocking.

"To hear you speak you'd think I was out of the contest altogether," he said at last. "But whether you like it or not, I'm the one who showed Brer Rabbit he wasn't the swiftest. And I'm the one to show Brer Bear here that he isn't the strongest, either."

The other animals roared with laughter.

"Come on, now, Brer Terrapin," said Brer Fox, choking with laughter. "Be reasonable. Just look at Brer Bear there, and take a look at yourself at the same time. Clever you may be, but strong? Why there's no question who is the strongest here."

"We'll see about that," said Brer Terrapin. "If Brer Bear is willing I'll prove it to you all."

"How are you going to do that?" asked Brer Rabbit.

"Give me a good strong rope," replied Brer Terrapin, "put me into the stream and then let Brer Bear try to pull me out."

The others began to laugh again.

"Oh that's too much for me, Brer Terrapin," said Brer Bear, wiping his streaming eyes. "Besides, we don't have any rope."

"You don't have any strength either," said Brer Terrapin. Then he lay back in the chair, closed his eyes, and rocked to and fro contentedly.

Brer Rabbit stopped laughing first. He had not forgotten his race with Brer Terrapin. "Right," he said. "I'll fetch a rope. Let's see who's telling the truth here."

Before long, Brer Rabbit was back, carrying a coil of strong rope under his arm and they all set off for the stream, led by Brer Terrapin. When he found the place he wanted, Brer Terrapin took one end of the rope and handed the other to Brer Bear.

"Now," he said, "you all go with Brer Bear into the woods and I'll stay here. When you hear me shout, that's the time for

Brer Bear to see if he can haul in the rope. If you take care of that end, I'll take care of this one."

Still laughing and joking, the animals followed Brer Bear into the woods. As soon as their backs were turned, Brer Terrapin dived into the water and tied his end of the rope firmly to a large tree root. Then he swam back to the surface and gave a shout: "Ready when you are, Brer Bear."

Brer Bear wrapped the rope round his hand and gave it a great jerk. Brer Terrapin did not even move. Then he took the rope in both hands and gave a long, strong pull. Still Brer Terrapin remained motionless in the middle of the stream. Brer Bear looked puzzled. He turned round, took the rope in both hands again and passed it over his shoulder. Using his whole weight he tried to walk forward with it. He could not move a step.

"Perhaps Brer Terrapin doesn't feel like walking today," said Brer Rabbit.

"Let me help you," said Brer Wolf. They pulled together.

"Let's all help you," said Brer Fox, and the animals gripped the rope and heaved together.

"Why don't you start pulling?" shouted Brer Terrapin. "I can't wait here all day."

The animals pulled and tugged and puffed and panted but Brer Terrapin did not move one inch from his position in the stream. At last Brer Terrapin felt the rope go slack and he knew that they had all fallen down with exhaustion. Quickly he dived down to the root, untied the rope and swam back to the edge of the stream. By the time the others had panted back to him he was sitting there holding the rope with one hand as if he had never let go of it.

"That last pull was a mighty stiff one," he said. "Just a little more effort and you'd have got me. You're certainly a strong one, Brer Bear, you pull like a couple of bullocks. But I just had that extra little something today." Brer Terrapin gave Brer Rabbit a very interesting wink. "Now, who else wants to test my strength?"

Brer Rabbit meets his match

One year Brer Rabbit and Brer Buzzard joined forces, sharing the costs of seeds and later the harvest of vegetables they grew on their land. Brer Rabbit was put in charge.

It turned out to be a very good year indeed. The rain fell at the right time and the sun shone just when it should and the vegetables all grew big and fat and delicious. But, strange to say, when Brer Buzzard called on Brer Rabbit to discuss sharing out the crop, there were no vegetables to be seen. Brer Rabbit was sitting there moaning about how hard times were.

"It's all right for you, Brer Buzzard," he said. "You can sleep in any tree you like. You've got your independence. But look at me, I've a house to keep up, to say nothing of my wife and all the children. How we are to survive the winter I'm sure I don't know."

Brer Buzzard said nothing but went away and thought a very great deal. One day a few weeks later he came back to Brer Rabbit's house.

"Brer Rabbit," he shouted, "are you there? I've some good news for you."

"What's that, Brer Buzzard?" asked Brer Rabbit cautiously.

"I've found gold on the other side of the river. There's a rich mine there, I can tell you. Come along with me, Brer Rabbit. I'll dig and you can sieve and between the two of us we'll soon get rich."

Brer Rabbit was only too eager to get to work but there was one big problem.

"How am I to cross the river, Brer Buzzard?" he asked. "If I get even a paw wet the whole family catches cold. Obviously I can't swim across."

"I'll carry you over on my back," said Brer Buzzard. "Just wait until we get to that gold mine."

So Brer Buzzard squatted down, spread his wings so that Brer Rabbit could climb up and took off. With Brer Rabbit clinging tightly to his feathers, they climbed up and up. Brer Rabbit kept his eyes shut. After what seemed hours they landed. Brer Rabbit opened his eyes a crack and looked down— and down and down. For Brer Buzzard had landed right at the top of the highest pine tree and the pine tree was growing on an island and the island was in the middle of the river with deep water swirling round its banks.

Brer Rabbit was certainly not stupid and he realized at once what was happening. By the time Brer Buzzard had balanced himself on the branch Brer Rabbit knew what to do.

"While we are resting here for a moment, Brer Buzzard," he said, trying to stop his teeth from chattering, "I'll tell you a secret. I've a gold mine of my own back home— one that I made myself. Perhaps we'd better go and see about that one before we bother with yours!"

Brer Buzzard laughed until every feather shook.

"Hold on, Brer Buzzard," screamed Brer Rabbit. "Don't flap your wings when you laugh. If you do something may fall off your back and then my gold mine won't do you any good and yours won't do me any good either. Let me down now and I promise . . ."

But Brer Buzzard was a tough old bird and he did not let Brer Rabbit down until he had told him exactly where the crop was hidden and promised to divide it fair and square. Then at last Brer Buzzard swooped down to the ground again and Brer Rabbit jumped off safe and sound. But Brer Rabbit's knees didn't stop trembling for a good month afterwards.